Dean Duffy

ALSO BY RANDY POWELL

Three Clams and an Oyster

Run If You Dare

Tribute to Another Dead Rock Star

The Whistling Toilets

Is Kissing a Girl Who Smokes Like Licking an Ashtray?

My Underrated Year

RANDY POWELL

Dean Duffy

A Sunburst Book   Farrar Straus Giroux

Copyright © 1995 by Randy Powell
All rights reserved
Distributed in Canada by Douglas & McIntyre Ltd.
Printed in the United States of America
First edition, 1995
Sunburst edition, 2003
1 3 5 7 9 10 8 6 4 2

Library of Congress Cataloging-in-Publication Data
Powell, Randy.
    Dean Duffy / Randy Powell. — 1st ed.
        p.   cm.
    Summary: Eighteen-year-old Dean, a former high school baseball
star whose future has been ruined by a batting slump and a bad arm,
is offered a college baseball scholarship and finds himself uncertain
of whether to take it.
    ISBN 0-374-41698-2 (pbk.)
    [1. Baseball—Fiction.   2. Self-esteem—Fiction.]   I. Title.

PZ7.P8778De 1994
[Fic]—dc20

                                                94-29037

For my wife, Judy,
and for my sons, Eli and Drew

Dean Duffy

One

MY TEN-YEAR "CAREER" as a baseball player ended in May of my senior year. It was the last game of the season, a home game, eighty-six degrees, dust swirling around the infield. At the bottom of the ninth, we trailed 3–13, which was the same as our win–loss record that season. I was at bat with two outs, nobody on base, and only three spectators left in the stands.

The pooped pitcher was throwing me fastballs right down the middle. I kept fouling them off, pitch after pitch. The count stayed 1 ball and 2 strikes. It was my 77th at-bat of the season. I was 4 for 76 for a batting average of .052, which was why the opposing pitcher was throwing me chest-high fastballs.

I knew this was the last at-bat of my life, and I pretty much just wanted to get it over with. But I wasn't quite ready to commit suicide. I still had my hitter's savvy, and it told me the next pitch was going to be a change-up.

And sure enough, along comes this big fat lazy moonball. I cocked my bat, waited for the ball to float its way to me, and I swung for all I was worth. And missed. I turned and looked in disbelief at the ump, who nodded and raised his mask and said quietly, "It's over, Dean."

And so it was. The end of baseball and the end of a dream I had devoted my life to since I was seven years old. As I walked to the dugout, I held my head up and did not drag my bat.

A few days later, another lifelong career ended: school.

Our graduation ceremony was held at the Seattle Center Arena, followed by an all-night dance in the Alki Room of the Seattle Center, music provided by a heavy-metal band called Flex. Throughout the night, I said goodbye to my classmates, and the next day my parents, three kid sisters, and I moved from our house in a north Seattle suburb to a dilapidated wreck of a farmhouse on San Juan Island in northern Puget Sound, four hours away from Seattle.

It was on a gorgeous piece of greenery, with broad pastures, horses, a sweeping eastward view of the sound, a fresh stream running along the back boundary. My folks had quit their jobs and sunk their life savings into it and planned to renovate the house, turning it into a bed-and-breakfast. For the past twenty-seven years, Dad had been the head maintenance man at the Nimbus Creek Golf and Country Club, and Mom had held var-

4

ious cleaning jobs. Now they were going to make their living catering to Seattle yuppies who wanted a weekend getaway.

I wasn't sure what I'd be doing afterward, but that house was my summer job, and I threw myself into it. My dad and I worked fourteen hours a day seven days a week. My three sisters fed the horses, and my mother fed us.

I spent more time on the roof and ladder than on solid ground. Day after day, the sun beat down on me. It was just what I needed: hammering, patching, scraping, painting, sweating. My skin turned brown; my dark hair grew down over my shoulders: I looked like Tarzan or Conan the Barbarian.

The work had its own rhythm and pace. It didn't quite compare to shooting strikes past a batter or ripping a base hit into the opposite field with a runner in scoring position, but it was satisfying in its own way.

Baseball, that nightmare, was behind me, and I needed to look ahead to what I'd do next. College, of course, was the most likely prospect. Although I'd been accepted to the University of Washington in Seattle, I wouldn't be able to attend until I could find a way to pay for it, which meant filling out every financial-aid form I could get my hands on, along with finding a job and saving some money. I knew I should have been preparing sooner, but right up to the spring of my senior year I'd had good reason to believe I'd be offered a baseball scholarship somewhere. This was no delusion, believe me. But in the end it had all fizzled out.

I worked straight through summer, on into September, one of the hottest and driest on record. There hadn't been a drop of rain in the Pacific Northwest since early May.

One Friday afternoon toward the end of September, I finished painting the exterior of that gigantic house. Two coats' worth. I climbed down the ladder and walked around "Duffy Inn," admiring my work.

The four guest rooms were still three months from being ready for guests, but reservations were already trickling in. After this weekend, they'd be coming in faster, because *Pacific* magazine was sending a crew out to do a "Before and After" feature on our place. My folks were going to get some free publicity.

I figured it would be a good weekend for me to get away, go back and visit my old neighborhood just north of Seattle. I could stay with Jack and Shilo Trant in nearby Nimbus Creek. I hadn't talked to them for two weeks or seen them since graduation, and I missed them more than any friends my own age. I had known them since I was seven, when I had become friends with their son, Van. Van and I had stayed halfhearted friends, while Jack Trant and I had grown close. It was Jack who'd discovered my talent for baseball, and for the past ten years he had been my coach, trainer, mentor, and second father.

That Friday afternoon, after I finished looking over my paint job, I stood at the kitchen counter, studying the ferry schedule, when the phone rang.

"Duffy Inn," I said.

"Hey there, Dean Duffy. You sound more like your old man every day."

I smiled. It was Jack Trant.

"How's painting?" he asked.

"Finished," I said. "A few hours ago. The whole mess."

"No kidding. Way to go, pardner. What're you up to now?"

"Looking at the ferry schedule."

"Oh?"

"I was thinking I might call you and invite myself over for the weekend."

"Don't bother. You're invited."

"Hey, thanks."

"Don't thank me. It's that wife of mine. She misses your homely kisser."

My smile broadened. "I miss hers, too."

"There's a couple of things I want to talk to you about," Jack said. "Not now, when you get here. Let's just say they have to do with your future."

"I'm open for suggestions," I said.

"Good. And dust off your golf clubs and bring 'em along. There's a man I want you to meet. Dick Drago."

"Dick Drago?"

"An old friend of mine. Fraternity brother. He's just passing through town tomorrow. We have a tee-off time for one o'clock. Me, Dick, Shilo . . . and we need a fourth. How about you?"

I wasn't sure I had heard right. "The fourth? In your foursome?"

"Think you can handle that?" he said.

"Playing? Not caddying?"

He laughed. "I said bring your clubs. That means playing, not caddying."

"Who's Dick Drago?"

"I told you, an old friend. Can you be here by eleven?"

"Easy. The first ferry leaves at six."

"Thataboy."

As usual, Jack hung up without saying goodbye. I pressed my palms on the cool surface of the newly installed kitchen counter, then folded the ferry schedule and stuck it inside my wallet.

Two

EARLY SATURDAY MORNING I drove my '63 Volvo onto the eastbound ferry, which took ninety minutes to go from San Juan Island to Anacortes on the mainland. From there, it was a two-hour drive to Seattle.

The evening before, when I had told my parents about Jack's golf invitation and about how Jack wanted to talk about my future, my mom had given my dad an I-told-you-so look. "See?" she'd said. "Jack hasn't given up on him. Just because the baseball didn't work out, Jack Trant is not going to leave Dean high and dry." Then Mom had turned to me. "Who's this Dick Drago?"

I'd shrugged. "No idea."

I had one stop to make: my old house. It was in a

suburb twenty miles north of the Seattle city limits but still considered part of greater Seattle. I drove through the old neighborhood and pulled up in front of my house. I sat looking at it with the motor idling.

A tricycle had been left in the driveway and a toy fire engine on the first step of the porch. The lawn needed a mow.

I looked up at my old bedroom window, not sure what I hoped to see. My ghost, maybe. The ghost of that Dean Duffy who used to stand at his bedroom window, fingering and fingering the seams of a baseball, pounding the ball repeatedly into his glove.

I'd had an unhittable fastball and a natural batting swing from the time I was seven years old. That was the year Jack Trant had taken me to my first Little League tryout. When the coaches saw my physical size and throwing speed, they weren't about to let me pitch to seven-year-olds; they made me turn out with the ten-year-olds.

I had met Jack a few months before that. His son Van and I were in the same first-grade class, and I had gone over to Van's house a few times. Also, Jack had been a member of the Nimbus Creek Golf and Country Club for almost as long as my dad had worked there, and they knew each other well.

Jack was a celebrity. He had played baseball at the University of Washington in the early 1960s and had pitched eight good seasons in the big leagues before retiring at his peak. Now he owned a medium-sized construction company, but spent most of his time on the golf course, or as a booster for the UW, helping his old alma mater recruit high school athletes. He loved all sports, but especially golf, fishing, baseball, and football—in that order. Four or five times a year he was a guest on one of the local radio sports talk shows. Occasionally he gave gruff motivational talks to school or church groups.

By ninth grade I had reached six foot three; by tenth, six-four. That was as tall as I got, but it was tall enough to make college recruiters and pro scouts take me very seriously when I was a mere sophomore. Especially with Jack Trant coaching me.

Jack had always said I had the kind of talent that needed a minimum of coaching. I had the dedication to match the talent. Ninth grade, my last year of junior high, I was brought up to hit and pitch for the high school varsity. A ninth-grader mowing down upperclassmen with split-fingered fastballs, forkballs, off-speed change-ups, sliders, wicked curves. Then stepping up to the plate and slugging the ball to all fields.

My sophomore year, Jack arranged for the University of Washington to give me a card that was like a key to the campus. It was purple with a gold R on it that stood for Recruit. What a huge part of my life that card was for a year or so. I still carry it around in my wallet, even though it expired a long time ago.

Spring of my sophomore year, the major leagues came to see me. The scouts sat in the bleachers taking notes; I always knew when they were there. That spring I struck out ten batters per game, hit .587, was the only sophomore in the state chosen to the Seattle *Times* High School All-State Team.

But then it all changed. The dream died, and I was still trying to figure out why.

A face appeared in the upstairs window. Not Dean Duffy's ghost but the new owner of the house, not pleased at the sight of a long-haired kid in a beat-up Volvo staring at his home.

I shifted into first and drove away.

Five minutes later I was entering Nimbus Creek, where Jack and Shilo lived. Nimbus Creek was two miles north of my neighborhood, which was why Van Trant and I had gone to all the same schools, including Nimbus Creek High. But socially our neighborhoods were very far apart. Nimbus Creek was really a kind of small town with its own chic shops and strip malls. I guess you'd call it a "community." The entrance to the residential area had a cascading man-made waterfall, an island of flowers, and a cheerful sign that said *Welcome to Nimbus Creek—Speed Limit 20 MPH—Slow—Children at Play*. Every fifty feet or so were speed bumps and brightly painted crosswalks with signs reading *Caution—Golfers Crossing*. One of the best private golf courses in the state, Nimbus Creek Golf and Country Club wound its way through a maze of cul de sacs. More than half the houses in Nimbus Creek were built right on the golf course.

Although it wasn't a town, Nimbus Creek had its own police force: two unmarked sky-blue police cars, usually parked at the doughnut shop or lurking behind bushes to catch speeders.

I drove into the Trants' cul de sac and parked in their upward-sloped driveway. I left my keys in the ignition and my clubs in the trunk. I rang the doorbell.

Jack opened the door. "Good man, you're early. Got your clubs?"

"Yep."

We shook hands. Jack spent a large part of his life shaking hands. He always squeezed my hand as hard as he could—either to test my grip or his.

Jack was fifty years old. He was a couple of inches taller than I, and a whole lot burlier. The past few years, his stomach had started to hang over his belt. Too many steaks on the barbecue and beers at the club.

His arms were like trees. He could drive a golf ball 360 yards. Shilo could drive one about half that far but was less likely to hook or slice it, which was why she beat Jack more often than he cared to admit.

"Let's talk before Drago gets here," Jack said, heading toward the kitchen.

"You going to tell me who he is?" I said.

Jack kept walking. "Didn't I already?"

Shilo joined us. "Dean, my goodness, you're so tanned! You look like—like mocha."

Shilo's voice was soft and slightly hoarse. Call it sexy. A voice dirty old men pay to hear when they call 900 numbers.

She opened her arms wide and gave me a hug.

She was holding a can of Pledge and a beige rag that I recognized as the long-sleeved shirt Van had bought one summer afternoon at the Pike Place Market. Shilo had evidently been polishing everything wooden in sight. She was wearing a jogging outfit the same color as the Nimbus Creek police cars.

Beautiful, broad-shouldered, athletic, Shilo was Jack's second wife, fifteen years younger than Jack. She had become his housekeeper a couple of years after his first wife, Van's mother, had left for good.

If Jack had always been my ideal father, Shilo had

always been my ideal mother. She never raised her voice, never nagged. In addition to golf, she shot a great game of pool, was involved in school and charity and community stuff, knew all the checkers at the supermarket on a first-name basis, and always made sure to ask me how my parents were doing. She could even remember the names and current ages of my three sisters, which was more than I could do.

She and another woman, an older friend of hers, owned a little boutique that dealt exclusively in tennis outfits for junior misses. Her friend's name was Champagne. They called their shop Champagne and Shilo. Mothers paid ludicrous prices for designer tennis dresses for their little tennis bimbos.

Air-conditioning was blowing through vents in the floor, and New Age music was being piped through built-in ceiling speakers. The house was as pleasant as one of Shilo's hugs.

We sat down at the kitchen table. As sunshine streamed into the kitchen, golfers passed by outside. The Trants' house was on the seventeenth fairway. Occasionally a golf ball would come rolling right up their back yard and under the deck, and a golfer would slink up there to retrieve it. A two-stroke penalty.

I used to caddy at this golf course. Every morning of every summer for seven years. It was about the only thing I ever did regularly that wasn't baseball-related. I was a good caddy and made decent money in tips. When Jack played he'd always reserve me for himself or for one of his VIP friends. Then he'd brag to them about me, about what kind of future I had as a baseball star and how I'd always been like a son to him. Since it came from Jack Trant it carried some weight, and those big-shot friends of his would treat me more like Jack's son than like a caddy, and slap me on the back and give me a huge tip and say, only half jokingly, "Remember me when you're famous, kid."

The golf course brought back a lot of good memories, and one of the best of those was Stewart Pitts. Pitts had caddied here for three summers—sixth through eighth grade. We'd been classmates since fourth grade but had never actually been friends until those summers. On Monday mornings, caddies were allowed to play free, and Pitts and I would play eighteen, sometimes thirty-six holes together. On rainy days, we were often the only ones out on the course. We didn't say much and never saw each other outside the golf course, but we seemed to really enjoy each other's company. Pitts had a way of making me feel that life was very simple and easy, something you could cruise right through, nothing to get worked up about.

For some reason, during the past few weeks I had found myself thinking about Pitts from time to time, even though he and I had long since gone our separate ways. Back in ninth grade, Pitts had done what adults called "falling in with the wrong crowd"—the stoners —and he had quit caddying and playing golf. In high school, we were strangers. Sometimes I'd pass by him in the hall, and I'd find myself wanting to stop and talk to him. I had always felt like Pitts *knew* things, like he had common sense and a sort of quiet wisdom, no matter how much he numbed it with pot. I never did stop and talk to him, but I often wished I had, and I kept thinking that maybe someday, when the time was right, I'd look him up.

Jack poured himself a cup of coffee and heaped in

three spoonfuls of Coffee-mate. I had a fresh lemonade with ice cubes; Shilo, a diet cola.

We talked for a while about my family and the house. It was the kind of small talk that is meant to lead to something.

"How about telling me a little more about this Dick Drago?" I said.

"Not much more to tell you," Jack said, looking away from me. "He and I go all the way back to fraternity days."

"What does he do?"

"Do? Works over in eastern Washington."

"You wanted me to meet him for some reason?"

"No real reason," Jack said, shrugging.

There was a short, strange silence. Then Jack cleared his throat. "But listen, son, that's not what Shilo and I wanted to talk to you about. We have an offer for you."

"An offer?"

"Ned and Rose Whittick are leaving for Europe next week. You knew that, didn't you?"

"Sure, I knew they were going," I said. "I didn't know it was next week."

"Well, they have a little apartment in the University District. They want somebody to apartment sit. The person they had backed out at the last minute."

"They need someone reliable, Dean," Shilo spoke up. "Someone to water the plants, keep the place in order. Keep things dusted off, feed the fish, collect the mail. You know how fussy Ned is about all his . . . things."

"Fussy?" Jack snorted. "Hell, he's worse than an old woman."

I had known Ned and Rose for years. Rose was Champagne's daughter. She was about three years older than I and we'd been occasional companions over the years.

"Apartment sit," I said. My first reaction was disappointment. Not for myself, but for Mom. She'd been so excited about Jack's wanting to "talk," figuring Jack and Shilo had some big plan for me—and here the big plan was only to hang out for a season.

But I liked the idea of being on my own for a while, with no real responsibilities other than watering Ned's plants and such. Of course, I'd have to find some kind of job and start putting money away. Also, it was time to collect all those financial-aid forms and come up with a game plan for the rest of my life.

Then Jack threw in a sweetener. He could give me a part-time job. He said he had something perfect for me, but he'd tell me about it later.

We agreed that I'd talk to my folks about it when I got home on Sunday evening. If they gave the okay, then I'd meet with Ned and Rose early next week to go over the details. As for the part-time job—

"Don't even think about that right now," Jack said. "Let's just take one thing at a time."

"I think it'll be great for you, Dean," Shilo said. "We'll get to see more of you." She gave me a warm smile.

"Darn right," Jack said. "I want you in town this fall. Who would I go to Husky football games with? Shilo goes on the nice days, you go on the lousy ones. Just like always. And we'll play some golf, too. And do some fishing."

"You guys are great," I said, and meant it. I took a sip of lemonade, but there wasn't any left, and an ice cube thunked my upper lip.

We were silent for a while, the only noise being the piped-in music and the low hum of air-conditioning.

Then, suddenly noticing my empty lemonade glass, Jack pointed at it. "Say, honey. This kid needs a re-fill."

Three

DICK DRAGO SHOWED UP at 12:15, looking cool from having been sealed inside his air-conditioned Ford Taurus rental car. I greeted him at the front door, since Jack and Shilo were still upstairs changing into their golf duds. Drago's expensive-looking black golf bag banged the doorway as he carried it in by the strap. He leaned it against the wall, and we shook hands.

He was a big man, approximately Jack's build and age, and I had the distinct feeling that he was a former baseball player. I have a sense for ball players. They have a certain manner that can only come from years of shagging fly balls on lazy spring and summer afternoons. I suppose other sports have their own auras, but baseball's is the only one I can detect.

Was he a former teammate of Jack's? Surely I would

have heard of him from Jack, although Jack had so many old baseball friends, there must've been plenty he'd never told me about.

Drago had big freckled arms covered with reddish hair, a bushy red mustache, and a balding freckled head. He was wearing an expensive wristwatch and a wrinkled white sport shirt that had come untucked in the back. His athletic shorts exposed muscular, hairy thighs; his white socks were pulled up to his calves.

He looked at me as though he were doing his own sizing up. I met his stare without flinching—one of the skills you acquire from years of stare-downs with hitters and pitchers.

Jack and Shilo descended the stairs. Jack was wearing purple shorts with the UW Husky logo on them. Shilo was behind him with her hands on his shoulders. She paused to straighten a picture on the wall, maybe just to give Jack some distance so that she could make her own entrance. She was a sight in her black tank top and khaki shorts.

Jack and Drago shook hands with genuine feeling. Shilo seemed to like him, too. She blushed when Drago kissed her. Who the heck was this guy?

It came out in the conversation that Jack and Drago hadn't seen each other for four years, although during that time they'd occasionally talked by phone. They patted each other's stomachs, each commenting on how well the other appeared to have been eating.

The four of us headed for the golf course along the pedestrian path that meandered through Nimbus Creek. It was a ten-minute walk to the clubhouse from the Trants' front door. The two friends caught up on old news, while Shilo and I walked behind them. Drago and I carried our golf bags; Jack and Shilo kept theirs at the club locker room. Of our four pairs of shorts, mine were the only ones that came down to my knees.

The men's locker room was a gray-carpeted club within a club. Jack was as popular here as anyplace he went, and his gruff voice and burly laughter echoed throughout the locker room. Allowing himself to be introduced to everybody, Drago was polite but reserved. Jack didn't have to introduce me, since I had caddied for a lot of these men and all of them knew my dad. One after another they came up to me, slapped me on the back, asked how my dad was doing, and told me to say hello for them.

Since it was Saturday, the golf course was crowded and the tee-off times were stacked up. Out on the first tee, there was a large crowd of spectators. Also, the restaurant was filled for lunch, and most of the tables had a view of the first tee.

Waiting for my turn, I was plenty nervous, with all these spectators. I wished I had gone to the driving range a few times that summer.

Jack went first, hit a beauty, long and straight. He was pleased and didn't try to hide it.

"Let's see you beat that, Deadeye," he said to Drago.

Drago pulled his golf glove onto his left hand, teed up his ball, and after taking two smooth practice swings, hit a perfect drive that rolled right up to Jack's ball.

My turn. The fact that both Jack and Drago had hit beautiful drives didn't ease the pressure I felt. Flubbed drives not only have a way of humiliating you, they dampen everybody else's spirits as well.

Carefully, I teed up the ball and measured it with the head of my driver. I tried to imagine myself stepping into the batter's box. Concentrate. You're at the plate, facing the pitcher. Relax. Smooth, easy swing. Don't try to hit it out of the ball park.

I felt the crowd watching me. I steadied myself. I could hear birds chirping and a sprinkler shushing somewhere. Somebody in the crowd struck a match.

Then I didn't hear anything. I saw only the ball, big and white, with hexagonal craters, and I swung through it and saw it shoot off low and straight, and I heard someone in the crowd say "Holy cow!" and I could still see the ball rolling up the fairway past both Jack's and Drago's balls.

There were whoops and applause from the crowd, and it took every muscle in my face to keep myself from grinning like an idiot. Jack, too, restrained himself, and simply gave me a nod.

While we watched Shilo tee off from the ladies' tee, Drago whispered to me, "Nice hit."

I was beaming inside. True, it was only one shot, but there was nothing like the feeling of hitting a ball—golf ball or baseball—right on the money and watching it soar away. It had been a long time since I'd had that feeling. A long time.

We all had a good round. Jack was hitting them straighter than usual. Drago's swing had a rhythm and timing that confirmed my feeling that he was an ex-baseball player. His chipping and putting were erratic, though; a visitor couldn't hope to know how to read the tricky greens of Nimbus Creek.

I, who hadn't picked up a golf club in months, managed to keep the ball on the fairway and not flub any shots. Being a former caddy and once-a-week player, I knew the greens almost as well as Jack did, and I sank some clutch putts for pars, and a long one for a birdie.

By the time we got to the seventeenth tee, we were within six strokes of each other. Jack had just birdied the sixteenth and was leading by four shots. With only two holes left, he was acting pretty cocky. "Hate to disappoint you, Dick," he said, grinning. "I just don't think you're gonna catch me today."

"Isn't he awful when he's winning?" Shilo said to Drago.

"I wouldn't count on it, Trant," Drago said. "I've seen you blow your share of ninth-inning leads."

Jack chuckled as he pulled his glove on with his teeth and drew his driver from his bag.

Shilo was leaning on her driver beside Drago. She gave him a nudge and pointed up the fairway to the right. "Look, Dick, you can see our house from here."

Drago peered ahead. "Ah, so you can."

She turned and smiled at me over her shoulder. "Hey, Dean, can't you almost picture Van out there in the back yard?"

"That's exactly what I was doing," I said.

"Van used to have these plastic army men he'd play with in the back yard," Shilo explained to Drago. "He'd be out there scooting around on all fours for hours on end."

"He had seventeen shoe boxes full of army men," I added.

"Hey, how about some quiet back there!" Jack snapped, interrupting a practice swing.

"Sorry, honey," Shilo said.

Van had done it for years, right up to tenth grade. He'd tried to get me interested in those "battles" of his, but I never had the imagination or the knees for it. When I'd be caddying for Jack and we'd be coming up the seventeenth fairway, Jack would avert his eyes from the strange-looking kid scrambling around the yard. When Jack wasn't there, other members I was caddying for would snicker and say, "There's Jack's kid."

Jack and Van never could get along. Van had a quick mind and a smart mouth and knew which of his dad's buttons to push. Shilo was the peacemaker; I was the neutral observer if I happened to be there.

Occasionally, Van and I would go bowling or to a movie, but Van didn't care a lick about doing the things Jack was interested in, and I did. So Jack and I did more and more things together and simply left Van out.

Back in August, when Van had gone off to college in Santa Cruz, he and Jack had not even said goodbye. They'd been fighting all summer about one thing or another. Now Jack paid Van's expenses, and that was about it.

I had always felt sorry for both Jack and Van. Jack, for having gotten stuck with a kid so far from the son he wanted, and Van for being so unacceptable to Jack.

"Just look at me," Van used to say to me. "I'm nothing but a cliché. The wimpy son who can't fill his macho celebrity father's shoes. It's so classic it's downright trite. Now you, Duffy, you'd have been the ideal son for Jack Trant. He wouldn't have named you after Grandpa Ivan; no, he'd have named you Jack Junior. Jack Trant

Junior—there's a name you could have hung your jock-strap on."

Plenty of times I'd wondered what my life would have been like if I *had* been Jack Trant, Jr. Better or worse, I'm not sure. Maybe having Jack as a real father would have put too much pressure on me. Maybe it's just not possible for a father and son to be the kind of friends Jack and I were.

Jack was taking way more practice swings than usual. When he finally teed off, his drive sliced miserably. In fact, it landed in his own back yard. If Van had been there, it might have pegged him.

"Two-stroke penalty," Drago said, trying not to smile. "Tough luck, Jack."

Jack flashed an angry look at his wife. "How the hell am I supposed to concentrate with you back there yapping?"

"Sorry, honey."

Jack took a nine on that hole, and a triple bogey on the eighteenth. He ended up in last place. Shilo won the whole thing and didn't rub it in as much as she normally would have.

Back at the Trants', we had iced tea and chips with salsa dip, and passed around the scorecard and talked golf. Although we were all hungry, we had only the chips, since Jack was going to barbecue some hamburgers. Then we went into the family room and flipped back and forth between two college football games. Shilo was in the kitchen, sculpting hamburger patties with those beautiful hands of hers. I felt at ease with Drago and was no longer suspicious of him, having decided he was just a friend of Jack's and nothing more.

Until, that is, Jack stood up and said, "I'd better see about firing up that barbecue."

I noticed Drago and Jack exchange a look. Drago said, "Sounds good, Jack. Like I told you, I have to leave for the airport right after the hamburgers. So maybe what I'll do is ask Dean here to go for a little spin and show me some of the neighborhood. Helps me wind down after a golf game. How about it, Dean?"

My eyes went from Drago to Jack. Jack's expression didn't change, but something in his face told me to go.

I turned to Drago and shrugged. "Be glad to."

Four

NOT SURPRISINGLY, we took Drago's air-conditioned Taurus instead of my beat-up Volvo. Drago backed down the sloping driveway, missing my car by about three inches.

We sat idling in the middle of the cul de sac.

"Great people, aren't they?" Drago said, tipping his head toward the Trants' house.

I agreed.

"Poor old Jack," he said, smiling and shaking his head. "You see the way he fell apart when Shilo mentioned his kid? Too bad that kid turned out to be such a disappointment to him."

"I guess Van always took after his mother," I said.

"Oh, I knew Tori," Drago said, nodding. "Very successful fashion model. Beautiful, but cold as ice. Wanted to be an actress. When she got pregnant, Jack talked her into having the kid. And, of course, kids have a way of changing your plans."

Not Tori's. She ran off to Hollywood, anyway, when Van was three, and never came back. Every two or three years, Van received a birthday card from her.

Drago and I were still idling in the middle of the cul de sac. The fan blasted cool air into our faces. It wasn't a bad place to be on a hot Saturday afternoon, but I would rather have been back in the Trants' family room, watching the fourth quarter of the Stanford–Arizona game.

At last, Drago shifted into drive and took off up the street to the stop sign.

"Point me in a direction," he said. "Let's see someplace that's special to Dean Duffy."

"Take a right," I said.

He gave me a glance and smiled. "That's what I like, a kid who knows where he's going. My line of work, I meet a lot of guys your age, I always say, 'Show me someplace that's special to you, someplace that'll tell me something about you,' and ninety percent of the time I get these shrugs and '*Gee, I don't know.*'"

His line of work? Guys my age? I stole a look at him as he sped up the street.

"Go straight through the four-way stop up ahead," I said. "But you might want to make a complete stop. Sometimes there's a cop hiding behind the bushes."

Drago took my advice. Then, easing through the intersection, we glimpsed the front end of a sky-blue cop car peeking out from behind the bushes.

"You're okay, Dean Duffy." For some reason, Drago

slapped his thigh when he said this. It made a sharp sound. Maybe he had wanted to slap mine but had thought better of it.

"How about handing me that sack back there?" he said, jerking a thumb over his shoulder.

When I gave it to him, he put it on his lap without opening it.

"You know," he said after a minute, "Jack and Shilo think the world of you." He drove casually, his right hand on the wheel, his left on his lap. "Jack's talked a lot about you over the years. I kind of feel like I've known you for a long time. He's darned proud of you. It may sound corny, but you've given him a feeling of accomplishment, you know. You're the son he wishes he'd had."

I said nothing.

"Anyway," he went on, "Jack called me a few weeks ago. Wanted me to meet you. I get a lot of calls from people wanting me to meet a kid. But when it's Jack Trant, you listen."

"Take a left up here," I said. My voice sounded small.

Drago turned, and we started climbing a steep winding hill. The car's automatic transmission hiccupped.

"What's that up ahead on the left?" Drago asked. "All that green. Looks like another golf course."

"Cemetery."

"Oh?"

"We're going past the cemetery to the top of the hill. There's a park up there—a baseball field."

"Good," Drago said. "I thought for a second you were taking me to the graveyard."

He had to stop for an old black dog who was sunning

himself smack in the middle of the street. The dog lifted his big head, blinked, yawned, his slimy tongue curling back, and went back to sleep. With a laugh, Drago eased the car around him. Jack would have honked his horn.

We passed the cemetery on our left. The black wrought-iron gates were open, inviting.

"Rest in peace," Drago said.

He still hadn't opened the sack on his lap. *You're okay, Dean Duffy*, he had said. As if giving me pluses and minuses on a scorecard. On my own scorecard I gave him a plus for his rental car and for not running over that dog. I gave him a minus for not opening the sack on his lap. And for saying things like *The son he wishes he'd had.*

I turned to him. "Who are you?"

He gave me a glance. "I guess I'm in management. And motivation."

I didn't try to hide my impatience. *"What?"*

He smiled. When we reached the park entrance, he had to slow down for speed bumps every thirty feet. The road circled the entire perimeter of the park. There were jogging trails, picnic tables, a wading pool, and a playground.

There was also a baseball field. It was used exclusively by the three high schools in the area, including mine. It was where I'd played my final game. And even though the last thing I'd done on it was strike out, the sight of that field gave me a rush of good feelings.

Drago parked the car in the ample shade, and we got out and walked to the ball field. He was carrying the sack with him.

"This is one nice ball park," Dick Drago said.

"Look at that grass," I said. "Perfect grass. And those dugouts. Real dug-out dugouts."

Drago looked at me and smiled. "You're excited. I like that. I wasn't sure you could *get* excited."

We sat down in the shade on the second row of aluminum bleachers. The aluminum felt cool on this hot day. Drago finally opened the sack. He pulled out two tangerines and tossed one to me.

"I was wondering what you had in there," I said, grinning.

For a while we concentrated on peeling and eating. Drago made a slurping sound. I studied a new callus on my hand that my golf club had made.

I pointed to right field. "See the home-run wall out there?"

"Yeah."

"See the hill behind it?"

"Yeah, I see it."

"Now, at the top of the hill there's a chain-link fence running along the ridge. See it?"

He squinted. "Yeah, barely."

"I parked one over that fence."

"Get outa here."

"It's true."

"A baseball?"

"Yeah."

"Ho ho," he said. "Gale-force wind at your back."

"No. No wind that day. Not even a breeze."

"How—how far is it?" he said. "Looks like it could be five hundred feet."

"From home plate to the fence it's five hundred and seven feet," I said.

"And you hit it *over* the fence?"

I looked at him and smiled. "And I was fourteen years old."

"Hey, come on."

"It's true. I hit it off a senior. A big-shot senior named Bean. I was a ninth-grader. It was only my third high school game as a freshman."

Drago was gazing directly at me, tangerine juice on his chin. "I know what you've gone through the last two years," he said. "I know the whole story. Are you through with baseball? Finished?"

I smiled, but it wasn't easy. "Finished."

"I'm a baseball coach," Drago said quietly. "Head coach. Shute College in eastern Washington. Ever hear of it?"

"Sure."

"It's a good small college. Private. Not much bigger than your average high school. But a top academic school. No baseball program, though. That's why they hired me last spring. One simple mission: 'Build a baseball program.' From ground floor, we're talking. They have a new board of trustees who want a nationally ranked baseball team in four years. And they're willing to put up as much scholarship money as it takes. I've been traveling all spring and summer, recruiting high school prospects. It's an uphill battle, even with our hefty scholarship fund. The really blue-chip kids have their sights set on the big schools—Arizona, USC, Texas. Faster track to the major leagues. A small school like Shute can't give them the exposure. So it's been tough, building a team, but we're getting there. We're getting there. We do have a future."

He paused, his eyes fixed on me. "Here's what I'm getting at," he said. "I want you to play baseball for me at Shute College this spring."

I went numb.

He continued in a low, gentle voice. "I know what it feels like, what you've gone through. I've gone through it myself. I know how it is to not ever want to *look* at a ball or bat again. You want another one of these?"

At first I didn't know what he was asking. Then I saw that he was holding open the brown paper bag of tangerines. I shook my head. He closed it.

"I have to admit," he said, "when I came here to meet you, I was more or less doing it as a favor for an old friend. I didn't think anything would come of it. That's why I wanted a chance to see you without your knowing who I was. That way, you wouldn't feel like you were auditioning. You wouldn't get your hopes up."

Drago spat in the dust, and continued. "You impress me," he said. "Just watching you swing a golf club, I saw something. Still, I've never actually seen you play ball. So I'm going by my gut feeling and by what I've heard about you, which is from Jack and a couple of sportswriters. Jack doesn't think you're washed up. He believes in you.

"Even so," Drago went on, smiling a little sheepishly, "I'm sticking my neck out. This is gonna be a tough one to justify to the athletic director. I mean, here I am, supposed to build a first-rate program, and I'm making an offer to a kid who batted .053 his last two years in high school."

".052," I corrected.

"Whatever," Drago said. "The A.D., she'll think I'm

loony. So I can't offer you much. What I can offer you is a one-semester scholarship. Tuition, room, and board. The semester starts mid-January. If you make the team, and if you have a promising season, I can extend the scholarship. Naturally, the better you do that first season, the more generous the extension. And, of course, if the baseball doesn't work out—I mean, if you don't make the team—you'd have to pay for your own education if you wanted to continue as a student. Shute's a private college, very, very expensive. And the classes are tough, whether you're on scholarship or not. There's no such thing as Mickey Mouse classes for jocks. You'll be up to your eyeballs in work. But you'll be getting a top-notch education.

"So that's my pitch," he said. "You chew on it. Talk it over with your parents, with Jack, whoever. I'll mail you all the application stuff. Like I said, second semester starts mid-January. You'll have to send in your application as soon as possible. If you get accepted, you'll have until December 13, no later, to decide whether or not to sign the letter of intent."

Similar to the slap he'd given his own thigh in the car, he now gave mine one. He glanced at his watch. "I have to turn in that rental and catch a plane in two hours. I'm seeing a catcher in Bakersfield. Any questions? Good. Let's go back and eat some burgers. I'm starving."

Five

WHEN DRAGO AND I got back to the house, hamburgers and corn on the cob were waiting for us. We ate in the family room while we watched a golf tournament that Shilo had taped on the VCR. Jack fast-forwarded through the commercials and occasionally switched to slow motion to analyze some pro's swing.

I was still dazed, but the hamburgers were good anyway.

When it was time for Drago to leave, we shook hands in the entryway. I thanked him. Jack put his arm around Drago and walked him out to his car.

My brain had always been slow at processing information. That was never a problem in baseball, where the body learns to react without thinking. But in life it kind of helps to think before you react, and for me, thinking took time and solitude and, ideally, a full tank of gas.

"What'd you think of Drago?" Jack asked me when he came back.

"He seems like a good guy. I think he's honest."

"He's that," Jack said.

"I don't think he really believed I hit that ball over the second fence," I said, smiling.

Jack chuckled. "Who does? You're the only one who —oh, never mind that. I'll tell you one thing about Dick Drago. He'll deliver on what he says. He'll be a heck of a baseball coach for Shute. You won't find a better man to work for."

I nodded. Jack and I were in the family room. From there we could look into the kitchen, where Shilo was noisily mixing milk shakes.

"He's made you a good offer, pure and simple," Jack said. "He told me about it while I walked him to the car. It's better than I expected. I didn't think he'd pay for a whole semester, including room and board. That's generous. He must've been pretty darned impressed with you."

"That's no surprise to me," Shilo said from the kitchen.

"Drago will make things happen at Shute," Jack said. "Give him three years. See what he does with that program by the time you're a junior, Dean."

Shilo brought in three fresh wild mountain blackberry milk shakes on a tray. After handing them out, she sat down with her legs drawn up.

We sipped our milk shakes.

"Shilo, this is great," I said.

"I picked the blackberries myself," she said. She had a milky-blue mustache above her upper lip.

"Good old Dick Drago," Jack said. "This is it, Dean. You've got yourself another shot."

"If he accepts," Shilo said.

"What?" Jack said.

"He's got another shot, if he accepts the offer. I mean, there *is* more to life than baseball, you know."

"Well, thank you very much for pointing that out," Jack said. He aimed the remote control at the TV and fast-forwarded through a set of commercials.

I sat there trying to think. Another shot. Ever since last spring, I had figured I was finished with baseball. Did I really want another shot?

A minute ago Jack had looked at me, full of pride and hope. I wished I could nod my head decisively and say, "You bet I'll take another shot." But I couldn't say it.

On TV, a golfer in plaid knickers was lining up a five-foot putt.

Shilo said, "Dean, you know you don't have to spend the whole evening with us."

"Of course not," Jack said.

"You probably have some friends you want to go and see," Shilo said.

I found myself nodding. I thought of Stewart Pitts, my old friend from caddying days. Why this craving to see him?

I stood up. "I don't know. Maybe I'll look up a few people. Maybe I'll just go for a drive and do some thinking."

"Drago wants you playing first base," Jack said. "Just like you did when you weren't pitching."

"We won't wait up for you, Dean," Shilo said. "Key's in the usual hiding place."

Jack clicked the remote control and killed the picture. "Doggone it, honey." He turned and faced Shilo.

"We've been through this, Jack," she said, closing her eyes. "We agreed last night we'd let Dean think this through in his own way. We agreed it would be best if we were noncommittal and didn't try to push him one way or—"

"Yeah, yeah, I know. Noncommittal," he grumbled. "You didn't sound so noncommittal when you said 'There's more to life than baseball.' "

"That's just because you were starting to push," Shilo said.

"Well, look, honey, I'm entitled to one speech. I'm going to go on record. It'll be the first and last damn speech I'll make about it. After that, I'll shut my mouth as noncommittally as you want."

Shilo smiled. "Go ahead. Go on record."

Jack turned to me and had to look up because I was still standing. "All right. Here's what I want to say. You thought you were washed up. Out to pasture at seventeen. But I've never for one minute believed you're washed up. The dream's still alive, son. If you decide to take this shot, it's not going to be easy. Some people will think you're crazy for turning out for baseball. You'll have all kinds of pressure on you, especially since you'll be on scholarship. But that's the way it should be. The pressure's good. When you're on scholarship, it means you're serious, you're at a whole new level of dedication and commitment. It's all or nothing. What I'm saying is, either take the scholarship and go all-out one hundred percent, or give up baseball for good. If you decide you've had enough of it for one lifetime, I won't blame you for a second. I mean that. But first you have to ask yourself one question, and you have to think long and hard about it, son, because the answer isn't going to come easy: Do you believe in Dean Duffy? That's the bottom line. And that's all I'm going to say."

Shilo was looking at him with a soft smile, and I could see there was a lot of love and tenderness in her eyes. "Not a bad speech."

I looked down at my feet. I tried to speak, but my throat seemed swollen. "Jack, thanks. I mean for calling Drago and for . . ."

I was going to say "everything," but it wouldn't have been enough.

"Yeah, yeah," Jack said, making a brushing-off motion with his hand. "Go on and get out of here. Don't come back before midnight. You need some money?"

Six

WHEN I GOT out to my car I was thinking more about Jack than about baseball or college, and my heart felt about as heavy as a hunk of lead. The sun had set twenty minutes ago, but the sky was still light.

It had been a long day.

I drove at a crawl's pace, with my window rolled down, and I stayed on streets where I wouldn't be tail-gated by other cars.

I knew that Jack was right about one thing: if I was going to continue playing baseball, it would have to be all or nothing, with my whole heart and soul thrown into it—just as it had been for the past ten years of my life.

I had figured this would be the first spring since I was seven years old that I wouldn't be playing organized ball.

Would I miss it? My favorite time of the year was early March, those first sunny days when spring is in the air and you're standing in the outfield during batting practice with the soft green grass under your feet and bees buzzing all around you and the girls' track team jogging past you and you're pounding your mitt and spitting and shagging fly balls and waiting for your turn at the plate.

Think of all the hours I'd invested in baseball. Hitting, fielding, throwing, pitching. All the hours Jack had invested, too.

In my mind, I was thinking Jack's words. *You thought you were washed up . . . The dream's still alive . . . People will think you're crazy . . .*

And Drago's: *This is gonna be a tough one to justify . . . I know what you've gone through the last two years. I know the whole story . . .*

The whole story. Drago knew *what* had happened, but did he know *why?* He couldn't. No one did, not even me. There was no explanation for what had happened my junior and senior years.

It started at the end of my sophomore year. That glorious season. When summer of that sophomore year came, I was invited to play for a newly formed team.

At first there were thirty of us. A diverse assortment of players selected from various high schools throughout Seattle. We knew one another only from the newspaper; we'd never even played on the same field. The only thing we had in common was that we were all fifteen years old, had all been invited to turn out for the team, and were all serious about baseball.

In other words, this wasn't your average Little League

team. And in other cities in Washington, Oregon, and Idaho, similar teams were being formed, and these were the teams we'd be playing that summer.

During June we had "training camp" six hours a day. Of the thirty players who had been invited to training camp, fourteen were cut, leaving a roster of sixteen. When the summer season began, we played three or four games a week and traveled by bus across three states.

Our sponsor was the Sara Chipman Funeral Parlor in Seattle. Our uniform colors were black and orange, like Halloween—orange hats with a black SC on them. Our nickname was the Gravediggers.

And the Gravediggers turned out to be something that summer. We had a chemistry. We ended up with a 22–2 record. We won the Western Counties Tournament, then the State Tournament, and then the Regionals in Corvallis, Oregon. On we went to the Nationals in Orlando, Florida—and we won the Nationals.

So, in September, we represented the United States of America in the International World Series, played that particular year in Lompoc, California. We beat Japan, Canada, Korea, Taiwan, and Puerto Rico, and we made it to the finals. In the finals, we faced a team that was being billed as the greatest in the world: Cuba.

The game was broadcast on satellite TV. Fidel Castro was said to have tuned in. I pitched and went the distance, a two-hitter. At the plate I batted three for four, knocked in two runs. We won three–nothing.

What a game. What a trip. What a summer. What a bunch of guys. Marty "the Buckmaster" Slayton, Tim "Moth Eye" Danielson, Leon "Toot Sweet" Wigmussa, Willie "the Smell" Garcia, Tyrell "Tugboat" Clubbs,

Elro "Wheelie" Garvasky, "Shampoo" Nickie Wainright, Larry "Chinook" Elwha . . .

What a bunch. God bless them all.

After the game, after we had showered and dressed, our coach, Norm Laddner, who sold insurance and had a huge square head, gave us a speech. It was the first time we'd seen him get choked up. "You bums," he said. "This is your last night together as a team. Go ahead, go out on the town. But do it with class. Get outa here! I love you bums!"

Wearing our black-and-orange Sara Chipman baseball caps, we hit the town and broke off into threes and fours like sailors on shore leave. Other players from around the world were doing the same thing on that hot, festive September night in Lompoc.

I and three others—Clubbs, Wigmussa, and Elwha—ended up with some girls. Four hometown Lompoc girls and four fifteen-year-old ball players from Seattle who'd won a ball game that afternoon. We played pool at a bowling alley until we got kicked out for rowdiness. We ended up at one of the girls' houses, her stereo blaring, dancing in our underwear, chasing one another around. That's all we did; it was perfectly innocent. We're not talking orgy or anything. They weren't loose girls any more than we were studs. But we knew we'd never see one another again, so we all went a little haywire for a night. We were good kids. Not angels, but good kids.

The four of us said good night to the girls, and then ran three miles to our hotel to beat the midnight curfew, which we did by two minutes.

The next morning we flew home to glory: parades, reporters, handshakes, shopping-mall appearances.

That day I had gotten out of bed with the usual all-around soreness that comes after pitching a complete game. But there was a pain deep in the elbow of my pitching arm, my left. A searing pain, as if a needle were being jabbed into the tissue. By the time I got home, I could barely lift the arm. I had to miss most of the hometown festivities.

The pain stayed. Fall and winter of my junior year ended up being a string of doctors' appointments. Creams, wraps, X-rays, therapies, ointments, exercises, pills, soaks, shots, medications, balms, more doctors, more specialists, more X-rays, endless talk of surgery. I swear Jack's hair started turning gray that fall. He used his influence with the UW athletic department to have me sent to their arm specialist.

After a barrage of tests, this doctor sat down with Jack, my parents, Coach Agbar, and myself. He fixed his eyes on me. "My good friend," he said, "you are sixteen years old. You have thrown one too many screwballs. You've thrown your arm out."

In early March the arm felt better. Back to the UW specialist for more examinations and questions. The main question, the one everybody asked, the only one that mattered: Should I attempt to pitch? The doctor finally said, Give it a try. But go easy. An inning or two. See how it feels.

We had a practice game against the JV team. Coach Agbar had me throw an inning of straight fastballs. Just fastballs. I told him the arm felt good. An hour later it was so sore I was begging anybody to whack it off. Agbar moved me to first base, permanently.

I could live with that. Pitching was my first love, but a bum pitching arm didn't have to affect my hitting. I'd be a hitter instead of a pitcher. Playing first base, no longer having to worry about pitching, I would put all my energy into hitting. Agbar had me batting in the heart of the lineup: number 3.

My first thirty trips to the plate resulted in a total of one hit. Agbar said to loosen up. Relax. You're still hung up about your pitching. But I couldn't buy a hit. Agbar moved me down to number 6 in the order. Then number 8. It broke his heart.

The doctors insisted that my sore arm had nothing to do with my batting swing. It was just a slump. Slumps, they said, are mental.

I finished my junior year with a batting average of .052.

The recruiters and scouts backed off. Even the University of Washington—despite Jack's influence. The scholarship offers that I'd always expected to come pouring in didn't.

But the dream wasn't dead yet. There was still senior year. I could still pull out of the slump, if I could only find the reason for it. There had to be a reason. Why the sore arm? Why the slump? Was I being punished for something I'd done? Was it a sign? A lesson I was supposed to be learning? There had to be *something* that I could find and correct in time for spring of my senior year.

In my mind I reviewed every bad deed I could remember committing. I supposed I'd done my share, but I just couldn't believe this was some form of justice or retribution.

I looked for other clues, and there was one incident that stood out as meaningful.

It was that last night in Lompoc, after we'd beaten

the Cubans, the four of us fooling around with those girls at the house. I had stepped out onto the back deck for some fresh air on that warm, starry night, alone, wearing only my boxer shorts. I heard their voices coming from inside, the pounding beat of the stereo, bursts of laughter. The song ended. For a few seconds, all was quiet except for the wind swooshing the trees. I looked up at the white clouds against the dark sky, with stars in between. I inhaled the scent of trees and grass. I held my breath, held it all in. It was a moment of absolute peace. I was holding in that day, not wanting to let it out. My entire future seemed to spread out before me. Don't get complacent, I told myself. Don't slack off. Keep working. Stay fixed on your goal. There will be plenty of moments like this.

But even as I was thinking that, my heart suddenly felt sad and heavy. I felt afraid.

And then another song started inside, somebody got pinched or tickled; Clubbs called my name. I rejoined them.

I had been driving for two hours and decided to head back to Jack and Shilo's. It was after 10 p.m. I would look up Pitts some other time.

Did I really want to put myself through another season like my junior and senior years? How could anyone still believe in me?

This time, if I failed, I wouldn't just be hurting myself. I'd be letting Jack down and making him look like a fool for recommending me to Dick Drago. And Drago would be a laughingstock, recruiting a guy who'd had two miserable seasons.

Hadn't the message been clear enough the past two seasons?

Forget about baseball. Find something else and get on with your life.

Still, it was there if I wanted it: one more shot.

Seven

THE SECOND WEEK of October, I moved into
Ned and Rose's apartment in the University District.

I was surprised that my parents had agreed to it so
enthusiastically. They both thought apartment sitting
was a great idea. They said I needed some time on my
own. It would help me come to a decision about Drago's
offer. In other words, they would support me no matter
what I decided, and they made it clear that the decision
was mine alone.

I appreciated this, but I also found it frightening.

The day I moved in was hot and dry. The drought—
"Indian summer," as non-natives called it—hadn't let
up. The apartment was all shut up and stuffy and sti-
fling, like a hothouse. It reeked of soil and plant fertil-
izer. The place was wall-to-wall vegetation.

I went around and opened every window that wasn't

permanently stuck shut. This only brought in a blast of oven-like air, along with traffic noise and exhaust fumes from University Avenue, or "the Ave," as it was called by locals.

It was the second week of school at the University of Washington, and from my fifth-story living-room window I watched students scurrying around with their University Bookstore bags full of new textbooks. I envied those freshmen, who were starting something new and important, but I wondered if they knew any more than I did about where they were going. Had they already made their big decisions?

I had just come from Sea-Tac Airport, where I'd joined Jack, Shilo, and Champagne in seeing Ned and Rose off to Europe. Ned was still giving me last-minute instructions even as he and Rose were being swept through the International Gate.

Prissy, fussy Ned. Rose was just the opposite, mellow and earthy. I liked her chubby moon face, her waist-long hair, those sultry, sleepy eyes.

Ned and Rose would be in Europe until December 20, and here I was, on my own for the first time in my life. Free and independent. No parents or kid sisters. A furnished bachelor pad right in the heart of the U. District—and no school. But my mom, before I left, had made sure to remind me that this was not a "vacation." "You'll be plenty busy," she said. "These could be the most important weeks of your life. You'll need to do some honest soul-searching. Your main job: figure out what to do with your life."

I cussed as I bumped my shin on one of the ten-speeds leaning against the wall.

Since the apartment was on the fifth floor, the living

room had a great view of the Olympic Mountains, but the best view was from the bathroom. Ned had told me that if you stood on the toilet and leaned out far enough through the small window, you could look down the alley and see Ravenna Park. I tried it, and sure enough, there it was, blazing with fall colors. The air in the alley was cooler than anywhere else, and I caught a whiff of real autumn. It felt like the first week of school. It fooled my heart into thinking that I was playing hooky and was supposed to be in school. But then I remembered I had graduated.

Ned had written notes on yellow Post-Its and stuck them all over the apartment. Everywhere I snooped, I found a note scribbled in his minuscule, ultraprecise architect's lettering. The notes gave me the creeps, as though the place were bugged.

On the kitchen counter I found a sheet of notebook paper, weighted down with a bottle of Linda's Plant Nutriment. On this paper Ned had written complicated, elaborate instructions for sorting the mail according to various "categories," watering the plants, feeding the fish, and "general housekeeping." He included a detailed floor plan of the apartment. A dotted line showed the route he took for watering the plants, and a dashed line showed the route he took for dusting.

Poor Rose.

I noticed an envelope on the kitchen counter. My name was scribbled on the front. Not Ned's writing.

I tore it open. It contained a handwritten note, a printed flyer, and a ticket. The note said:

"Dean, I think you'll get something out of this. Use it if you can. Rose."

The printed flyer was on green recycled paper. It was the kind of flyer you see stapled to bulletin boards and telephone poles, announcing a concert or event. It said:

An Evening with
RUTA WATERFALL
Annie Greenday Bookstore

The date was Friday—tomorrow night—in Wallingford, a neighborhood just west of the U. District. The ticket was good for one admission.

Who or what was Ruta Waterfall, and what was she going to do at the Annie Greenday Bookstore? And why had Rose thought I might "get something out of it"?

I put the ticket in my wallet and tossed the flyer and Rose's cryptic note into the cardboard box that Ned had labeled: "Junk Mail—Take Me Down Hall, Dump Me in Recycle Bin at Least Once a Week."

Maybe I could get something out of it, all right. Show up early and scalp the ticket.

Back in the living room I played a Pearl Jam CD. I wasn't crazy about Pearl Jam, but I wasn't quite ready to play something I was crazy about.

I began to dance around the apartment to the music, making sure I didn't bump my shin against any more bicycles or step on any plants. At first I felt self-conscious and kept looking around the apartment for hidden cameras. Gradually, I loosened up and began doing a sort of jazzed-up Chinook war dance.

In the bathroom I did twenty push-ups. Then, resting my cheek on the cool bathroom tile, I noticed something coiled in front of my nose. It was a single, unbelievably long strand of Rose's hair.

The living room seemed to be cooling off. A refreshing breeze was blowing through it. Outside, litter and leaves scuttled along the sidewalk. The blinds clanked. The calendar on the living-room wall fluttered and then fell to the floor with a splat. A cool, moist current of air was coming from the west—from Puget Sound and the Olympic Mountains.

Blackish-purple thunderheads were building a thick ceiling from Puget Sound to the U. District. The sun was gone; the sky had turned a luminous, eerie ocher.

Sparrows were tweeting like crazy. Then, suddenly, they stopped—everything paused—and there was a peal of thunder that rumbled away in the distance and rattled the windows.

Single drops of rain came. Plop. Ploomp. I stuck my hand out the window and felt them wet my palm.

Then the entire sky lit up with lightning, followed by a boommmmmmmm.

The sky opened. Rain came in torrents, bouncing so hard on the cement that it looked like watery static. Headlights came on, wipers became useless. People dashed every which way. Gutters overflowed. My hand and wrist got soaked.

The drought was over.

Eight

FOR THE NEXT FEW HOURS I played CDs and watched the rain. Traffic hissed and whooshed on the street below.

Around 8:30, Shilo phoned to see if I'd gotten moved in all right and to invite me over for breakfast tomorrow. I gratefully accepted.

The apartment gradually grew dark. I didn't bother turning on any lights.

What to do? The whole night was ahead of me. I could stay up all night if I wanted to. I could dance naked or look at dirty magazines or watch bugs or stare at the wall without being asked "What are you doing?"

I spent a few minutes staring at the wall.

What was I doing?

Don't start feeling lonely or homesick, I warned myself, sinking into an easy chair. You ought to have some human contact. You can't go isolating yourself. Where were all my friends? Most of them had gone off to college. Sure, I knew people who were going to the UW or to one of the community colleges, but why should I bother them? They'd be busy with school and with their new life. They'd ask me what I was doing, probably expecting me to say "Nothing," and I'd tell them I'd been offered a scholarship and they'd say something like "Wow! Great!" but inside they'd be thinking, "Who'd take him? Does he really think he can play college ball? How pathetic."

Well, maybe they'd think that and maybe they wouldn't. But they weren't the ones I wanted to see anyway.

Who did I really want to see? I sat up: Pitts.

What could Pitts do for me? Nothing. The guy was a loser; I could pretty much guess what he was doing. So why did he matter to me? After all the years of passing him in the hall without talking to him? Maybe because of those summers of our caddying and playing golf together. Maybe because they were good times that didn't have anything to do with baseball.

I got up and found the Seattle phone book in its most logical Ned-place—in the cabinet under the telephone. There were about forty Pittses, but only six had the correct suburban Seattle prefix. I wasn't sure what street Pitts lived on—I had never been to his house—so I had to call all six.

The first five were misses. I dialed number six. A woman answered.

"Is Stewart there?"

"Stewart? No."

"Does he, uh, live there?"

"Live here? Yeah, I guess he lives here. But he's out."

She explained that Pitts worked a graveyard shift, so he slept till four in the afternoon, and as soon as he got up, he'd grab something to eat and go off with his "buddies." And from wherever he hung out with his buddies, he'd go directly to work.

"Who are some of his buddies?" I asked politely, wondering if I'd know any of them.

"Oh, cheez, I don't know who Stewie runs with no more," she said. "I don't *want* to know. He's nineteen. He pays room and board. He don't have it so bad as he thinks. What was your name?"

I told her.

"Yeah, well, you tell me, Dean Duffy, some place in the real world you can get room and board for three hundred a month. That includes laundry. He don't have it so bad. It used to be three-fifty, but we knocked it down fifty because he takes Earlie for a walk every morning soon as he gets home from work. That's the time to catch Stewie, if you really want to catch him. When he takes Earl to Hamilton Park. He drives his car there. Right around seven-thirty, every morning. He can be dependable when he wants to be, although his father wouldn't agree with that. What'd you say your name was? I'll tell Stewie you called."

A couple of hours went by. Through the open window, I heard a gang of fraternity brothers marching down the Ave, chanting an obscene song to the tune of "Bye Bye Birdie."

I paced. Around eleven, I took a salami out of the refrigerator, smelled it, and put it back in the refrigerator.

Another hour passed. I didn't feel a bit tired. I decided I'd make my first night of apartment sitting memorable: I would stay up all night. In the morning, I could go and see Pitts.

Five minutes later, wearing my old letterman's jacket with the letter removed, I started walking down the Ave through the rain. There was an all-night 7-Eleven just ahead, but I had another destination.

It was a place called the Hasty Tasty. A sort of beatnik coffeehouse where college people hung out. Jack and I had gone a few times on Saturday afternoons, after Husky football games, when it always seemed to be raining. Sometimes Jack would park his car in the pay parking lot next to the Hasty Tasty and we'd walk to the stadium carrying binoculars and a thermos, even though it was a long rainy walk all the way across campus, and even though we could have parked in the coaches' lot because Jack had a special pass. But it was a pleasant walk across campus, rain or shine, and when the game ended, we'd walk back and have lunch at the Hasty Tasty.

I hadn't been there for a couple of years, but it used to be open twenty-four hours. I remembered that for a mere eighty-five cents you could buy a peanut butter and jelly sandwich the size of a T-bone steak. And they had a glass case filled with homemade pastries. My mouth watered at the thought of it, and I quickened my steps.

———

The place was packed, full of cigarette smoke and conversation and the clink of coffee cups.

Dripping wet, I approached the counter. Behind it, sitting on a tall stool, was a girl dressed in faded jeans and a baggy yellow V-neck sweater. She was reading a thick hardcover book propped on her lap, her knees pressed together to support the book. A menu was scrawled on a green chalkboard leaning against the wall, but the chalk was so smudged it was unreadable. The lighted glass case that used to contain homemade desserts was still there, only empty. No desserts, just a black cat stretched out under the lights.

I stood at the counter, waiting for the girl to look up. It took a long time. When she finally did look up, I was stunned. Her face was pale and beautiful. She had big brown eyes with dark rings under them, no makeup. Her dark hair was tied back. She was about my age, but tired-looking.

I pointed at the cat in the dessert case. "Is this all you have for dessert?"

Her expression didn't change. I realized I probably wasn't the first person to come up with that line.

"What happened to all the desserts?" I asked.

"They're over there."

"Over where?"

"There."

Her lips were full, shapely, and pink; for a long five seconds I couldn't stop staring at them. Then I saw that the sleeve of her baggy sweater had fallen back to her elbow, and she was pointing at a card table on the other side of the espresso machine.

I found my voice. "Do you still have peanut butter and jelly sandwiches?"

"Yes."

"Are they still eighty-five cents?"

"No."

"What are they?"

"A dollar five."

"What? A dollar five? That's an outrage." I pushed my soaked hair off my forehead and water squeezed through my fingers, drops of rain running down my neck. "I remember when they were eighty-five. Must've been before your time. How come you don't keep your desserts in the case anymore?"

"I really don't know."

"Is the cat alive?"

"Does it matter?"

I bent down and tapped the glass. The cat did not move, but I could see it breathing.

I stood back up.

"Give me a jelly and peanut butter sandwich."

"White or whole wheat."

I stared at her. "White. Of course."

"Of course."

"And I'll have a look at those desserts."

"You do that."

I went over to the card table, giving her a quick look over my shoulder. She'd gone back to her book. I strained to see the title, but couldn't. I lifted the clear sticky lid of the dessert tray, and selected an old-fashioned glazed doughnut. There were some sticky silver tongs, but I used my fingers. I put the doughnut on a piece of waxed paper and took it back to the counter. The girl turned a page of her book. I wouldn't have minded standing there and watching her for a while.

She looked up. "That it?"

"That's it. Oh, maybe I'll have a coffee, too."

"Regular or espresso?"

"What?"

"Regular or espresso."

I had never had espresso before, but I knew it was made with that silver machine next to the counter.

"Espresso," I said.

"That it?"

"Oh, sure."

"Three-fifteen."

I hesitated. "You didn't even add it up. You just plucked that number out of thin air."

"Would you like me to add it up?"

I paid her. I took my doughnut on waxed paper and wandered around the place. A few games of chess were in progress. I stopped at one of them and pretended to study the board and make an instant analysis of each player's position. I had never been good at chess, because I couldn't think fast or far ahead. Much less with someone waiting for me to do it.

I walked on. Scattered about on the tables were various newspapers attached to long wooden sticks, the kind they used to have in our high school library. Others were hung on a wooden rack against one wall. Even though there was a buzz of conversation, most of the people were alone, reading or studying. There was a fat girl wearing a beret, writing in her diary. As I passed by, she gave me a fierce scowl and covered the page with her hand, as if I'd been trying to read her writing, which I had. A college girl was arguing in whispers with two other girls, looking from one to the other and jamming her index finger into the palm of her hand—". . . sociability in inverse ratio . . ." One of the girls was nodding her head up and down, while the other, smoking a cigarette, stared dreamily up into outer space.

At a table in the corner sat a surly man with long black hair and a long scraggly tangled beard. He looked as though he'd been stranded on a desert island for twenty years. He was glaring at me. He motioned for me to come over to him, so I did. He smelled of earwax and potato chips.

"Did you call me a mutt?" he asked.

"No."

He held up two fingers in a V and jerked them toward his mouth. "Moke."

"What?"

"Moke."

"I don't moke," I said, and walked away. I sat down a couple of tables out of range of his smell, next to a window that looked out on the lighted alley.

At the next table, a guy and a girl were sitting across from each other. The girl had blond fluffy hair. Her back was turned to me. She wore a bright lavender ski jacket, which was one of the few bits of color in this drab, smoke-filled place. She was talking animatedly to the guy, who was facing me, and who was listening to her with a crazed, faky smile on his face, nodding, nodding, smiling, fake-laughing. She was telling him some boring story about her laundry or dentist or something. They were on a date. For a moment I envied them.

I ran my fingers through my wet hair. I looked at my reflection and then through my reflection to the lighted alley. I saw the rain bouncing off the cobblestones. The lights in the alley created shadows; the shadows made me feel lonely. I had gone on my share of dates. In spite of all the expense and hassle and pain and horror and game playing, dating had its moments. But it helped to go out with someone you liked.

As far back as seventh grade, I'd had my pick of girls. I did things with girls that I'm now ashamed of. I don't mean strictly physical things; I mean, the way I treated them emotionally. It hadn't bothered me to tell some girl I loved her and wanted to go steady with her. It was a game. After a few dates, I would forget about her and move on to another. This left a wake of not so happy girls.

I got progressively more wild until my junior year, when my arm went bad. I did not rule out the possibility that God was punishing me for my past treatment of girls. To be on the safe side, I stopped dating altogether. It wasn't so difficult, since most of the girls weren't speaking to me anyway, and since I was absorbed in baseball. I didn't even go to the senior prom.

The girl from the counter brought my sandwich and espresso. The espresso was in a tiny cup, not like the regular-sized cups everyone else had. The sandwich was as enormous as ever. I took a bite, and the bread and peanut butter and jelly all melted in my mouth. I took a sip of the espresso and winced. It tasted like bitter mud. I poured some sugar into it and tried it again. Now it was sweet mud.

Then the girl did something that surprised me. She

sat down at my table, across from me. Just like that. She watched me eat. The dark circles under her eyes made her look like a beautiful tired kid.

She lit a cigarette and dropped the match into a glass ashtray on the windowsill, where two or three flies were lounging on their backs with their skinny legs kicked up. She blew the smoke out the side of her mouth, a stream that hit the window and dissipated between us.

I took another gooey bite. The jelly was cool, the peanut butter creamy, the crust chewy.

"What are you doing?" she asked.

My mouth was jammed full with sandwich. "Eating."

The answer seemed to satisfy her. She didn't say anything, just continued smoking, looking around the place. Then she looked back at me. "How is it?"

I smiled. "Does it matter?" One point for me.

"I suppose you go to the U," she said after a while, in a bored tone.

"No," I said. "How about yourself?"

She shook her head while blowing out smoke.

"You live around here?" I asked.

She gave a quick nod, killed her cigarette in the ashtray, and got up and left. On her way back to the counter, she picked up a dirty dish here and there but passed up many more.

I sipped my espresso. Who was she? How did she live? Why had she sat down?

A few minutes later, by accident, I saw her smile. A fat guy, college-aged, wearing a dishwasher's apron, had come out from the kitchen eating a doughnut. He had the face of a stand-up comic or a smart-ass. He leaned a few inches toward the girl and said something to her that made her look up from her book and crack a bright laughing grin.

I would have paid fifty dollars to know what that guy said to make her smile like that.

I finished off my espresso, including the sugary dregs. I laid some coins next to my saucer for a tip. As I walked toward the alley door, I turned and glanced at the girl. The fat dishwasher-comedian was blocking her, but I saw her go up on her toes to peer over the guy's shoulder at me. I gave her a quick wave. She didn't wave back, but her eyebrows flicked up for an instant. Which was like a wave.

Nine

THE ESPRESSO and the hike back to the apartment had given me a boost. Instead of entering the apartment lobby, I took the stairs to the underground garage, got into my car, and drove into the rainy night.

So far, this apartment sitting was pretty good. Granted, it was only my first night, but it seemed to me that all sorts of new experiences were waiting to happen to me. It seemed to me I was finally going to start living. Yes, that's it, to experience life. Up until now, my only life had been baseball, and that was how it would be if I were to take that scholarship; I'd have to focus entirely on baseball, along with trying to stay afloat in my classes. Wasn't it about time I had a chance to find out what life was all about?

I drove from the U. District toward my old familiar

territory, staying on the wet dark residential streets, passing playgrounds, stores, and houses. I turned the radio off so I could think more clearly. You have a lot of thinking to do this fall, I told myself. That is your job. Or one of your jobs. It occurred to me that I should start as soon as possible working that part-time job Jack had offered me. If nothing else, I needed the money. I would talk to him about it later, at breakfast.

As I drove, it hit me how much last summer I had really missed this area—my old neighborhood and high school and Nimbus Creek and the golf course and all these surrounding neighborhoods. I was going to enjoy driving around this fall and discovering new parks and baseball fields, revisiting old familiar baseball fields and reminiscing. I liked driving at night when the FM radio signal was clear and strong, but I loved the days, too, the fall leaves, the overcast skies, the rain and mud puddles.

The drought from the summer had turned all the lawns and parks brown, which was my idea of eastern Washington. That was where Shute College was located, way over on the other side of the Cascades, near Walla Walla and Pasco, in flat desert land. They had only two seasons in eastern Washington: cold and hot. Both of them harsh, both dry. Hell, I'd be playing baseball in sizzling ninety degree weather. Hotter and dustier even than the day of my final miserable strikeout.

Yes, I had missed this place during the summer, and I would miss it even more if I went to eastern Washington. Maybe I belonged here.

I drove through the steady rain. At dawn I stopped at a 7-Eleven and bought a large coffee. The sky light-

65

ened to gray, and I rolled my window down and filled my lungs with the morning air.

It was still drizzling gently when I headed for Hamilton Park, to see if I could find Pitts.

I recognized his blue souped-up Torino. It was the only car in the parking lot of Hamilton Park. Its personalized license plate read: TRIP ON. His graduation tassel hung from his rearview mirror.

Pitts was sitting on a picnic table under a tree, smoking a cigarette.

We shook hands. His eyes were droopy. True, he worked graveyard shift, but those eyes had another kind of droopiness. Even so, he still had that look of quiet savvy I remembered about him.

"Duffy, you bum," he said.

"Played any golf lately?" I asked him.

"Oh, man." He had a stoner's chuckle: "Heh-heh-heh."

I sat down next to him on the picnic table.

"My old lady told me you called," he said. "What're you after, drugs?"

"No."

"Say no to drugs, huh? Heh-heh-heh."

"I've just been meaning to look you up," I said.

He gave me a dubious look before taking a long pull on his cigarette, scrunching up his face. He had a fuzz mustache, long curly hair, and a black leather jacket with zippers slashing every which way, like silver scars. The left shoulder was torn. His curly bangs came down over his eyelids, so that when he blinked his bangs twitched.

66

"I don't get too many people looking me up reason," he said.

"Well," I said, "I guess I have a reason, but it's pretty lame."

"Yeah? What is it?"

I took a breath. "You know something? I'm not even sure I can explain it. Or that it's worth going into right now. What've you been up to lately, anyway?"

Pitts kept his eyes on me for a couple of seconds. Then he shrugged. "Working. You?"

"Nothing much."

Pitts spat. We sat there for a while. The rain made a dull pattering sound. The tree over our heads kept us dry.

"I'm living in the U. District," I said. "Apartment sitting."

"Cool."

Pitts's puny dog was snuffling here and there, dragging its leash behind it through the wet grass. Pitts noticed me looking at the dog.

"Name's Earl," he said. "Earl Anthony."

"Like the bowler?"

Pitts perked up. "You've heard of Earl Anthony? Oh, man. You're the first person who— My parents'd fall down and worship you if they knew you'd heard of Earl Anthony."

"Why did you name your dog after a bowler from Tacoma?"

"I didn't, *they* did. It's *their* dog. Earl Anthony used to be their favorite bowler. Don't ask me why. It ain't even a real dog. It's a lump of fur balls. I had a real dog once. A black lab. Name was Outlaw."

...ed up and swooshed the tall black firs
...d the field. When I was a little kid, that
...scare me, until I learned to close my eyes
...the swooshing sound was a stadium full of
...ns.

... was a great dog," Pitts said, "but he was
pretty ...mn dumb. He used to chase squirrels in our
back yard. He'd spend all day sitting under the trees,
looking up, yelping. The squirrels'd sit up there in them
maple trees laughing at him, dropping nuts down on his
head. My dad used to say, 'That is one worthless dawg.'
That's about all my dad ever said when he came home
from work. Or else he'd say, 'Why don't you train that
worthless mutt.' "

Pitts stopped, as though his voice had caught. I could
tell something terrible had happened to Outlaw. I
wasn't in the mood to hear about it.

Then Pitts laughed suddenly, bitterly. He grinned a
twisted grin at me. His teeth were crooked and tobacco-
stained. He was waiting for me to ask about the dog.

"What uh . . . happened to him?" I asked.

"Outlaw? You know what that dog did? I took him up
hiking to Mt. Pilchuck, few days after I bought my Torino. About a year and a half ago. Anyway, it come time
to go home, and Outlaw wouldn't get back in the car. Just
plain wouldn't do it. He was running all over the place. I
called and called that dog, man. I chased him all over, but
he wouldn't let me catch him. Then it started getting
dark. He wouldn't come. I had to give up. I had to leave
my dog at Pilchuck. Next day I drove back up there, but
there wasn't any sign of him." Pitts swallowed hard.
"You ever hear of a thing like that, Dean?"

"No," I said.

"Of course," Pitts went on, "I knew when I got home my old man'd have something to say about it. Sure enough, he says, 'Well, it's your own damn fault for not training it. What'd you expect? All's you did was let it sit around all day and look at squirrels. Didn't I keep telling you to train it?' And the thing of it is, Dean, he was right. He was right all along."

We sat and looked at the rain. Leaves were scattered everywhere. Earl Anthony sniffed around and ate some grass and coughed and ate some more grass. The dog didn't look well.

After a while I said, "How would you like to come visit me at the apartment sometime?"

"What for," Pitts said.

"How should I know? A visit. There's a place that's open all night. It's got these giant peanut butter and jelly sandwiches for eighty—for a dollar five. I'll treat you to one. They weigh as much as one of Earl Anthony's balls—bowling balls."

Pitts laughed. He laughed until it turned into a hacking cough.

"Seen anybody else lately?" I asked after a while. "From high school?"

"Nobody you'd know."

We were silent, listening to the rain.

"Come to think of it," he said, "seems to me like I did run into somebody. Somebody asking about you. At some party."

"Asking about me?"

"Yeah, something like that. Lemme think. Man, I was so fried that night."

"It was at a party?"

"Yeah, just give me a minute."

I gave him a minute. He stared. For a second I thought he was falling asleep.

"Oh, well," I said.

"My brain's gone, man," he said.

"Where're you working, anyway?" I asked.

"TechnoStat Engineering. I just started there a month ago. It's just a scut job in the shipping department, pretty worthless, but they have this training you can take. A two-year course. You take it and you learn all this computer crap. Graphics and art and programming and all that. And if you pass the course, you get to work on video games. *Making* video games. And after you've worked your way up, you even get to design new games."

"Sounds pretty good," I said.

"Yeah. When I told my old man, he said, 'They'll have robots doing all that crap in five years. The only people who are any good at that computer crap is Japs and robots.'"

Pitts laughed harshly. "That's my old man for you," he said. "I'm gonna go for it, anyway. I figure I've put enough money into those dang video games, I might as well try and get something out of 'em. Maybe I'm finally starting to get tired of being a loser. How about you?"

"I was tired of it a long time ago," I said.

"I meant, how about you in general. How are you and everything?"

"I'm all right," I said. "I . . . uh . . ." I passed my hand through my hair.

"You what?"

"I might have a chance to play some baseball."

"College?"

I nodded.

"Scholarship?"

I nodded again.

"All right," he said.

"Thing is," I said, "I don't know if I'll do it."

"Why not?"

"Why not? I was in a slump for two seasons."

"Yeah, I know," Pitts said.

"I tried everything to break out of that slump. Every imaginable way. You know, when a guy's in a slump, everybody's got advice. And I listened to it all. I went to hitting coaches. I even saw a therapist . . ."

Pitts shook his head.

"I don't know if I want to keep making a fool of myself," I said. "That's what I don't know."

Pitts shook his head again. "Life is one damn bitch."

"I guess," I said, not looking at him.

"Hey," he said. "You wanna get high?"

"No."

"Why not?"

"Why should I? I never have before. I don't have much reason to start now."

"I only got a couple buds left," he said. "I been thinking I'll smoke up the rest of what I have and not buy anymore. My brain's so gone. Sometimes I can't even remember my—" Pitts stopped. "Hey!"

"Hey what?"

"Hey!" Pitts's face had brightened. "Hey, I remember. It just came back to me."

"What did?"

"That dude who was asking about you. At that party. It was one of those fraternity parties in the U. District, back in August. There was this guy, he'd heard me and my friends say we'd gone to Nimbus Creek High, and

71

he says, 'Any of you know Dean Duffy?' I said I did. And he starts asking me all these questions. What's Duffy doing. Where does he live. Does he party, get high—stuff like that."

"What'd you tell him?"

Pitts shrugged. "Not much. I told him I'd heard you moved up to the San Juans with your folks. Everybody knows that."

"What did he say?"

"Oh, man, he got this weird look on his face. He said something like 'I would like very much to see him. I have some things to say to him. If you see him, tell him that.' Something like that. It was weird, kind of spooky even."

"What was?"

"Everything. His voice, the look on his face. And he wasn't even drinking."

"What was his name?" I asked.

"Huh?"

"Did you get his name?"

Pitts stared. "Uh, yeah, I got his name. Oh, man. Seems like . . . it was something like . . . it was a long name."

"A long name?"

"Yeah, three names."

"Three names."

"Yeah. That book."

"What book?"

"That *book*, you know? The one about that damn duck with three names."

"A duck with three names?"

"Yeah—er no, wait, not a duck. A seagull. Yeah. A seagull with three names."

"A seagull with three names."

"Yeah."

I tried to remember a book about a seagull with three names. It took a while. "*Jonathan Livingston Seagull?*" I said.

"Whoa, that's it," Pitts said. "How'd you know that? I'm impressed, Duffy."

I stared at Pitts in disbelief. "*Bean?* Was that his name? Jonathan Livingston Bean?"

"Bingo," Pitts said. "Bean. Rhymes with Dean."

"I can't believe it," I said, shaking my head.

"Who is he? Man, you know your face went pale? Who is this guy?"

"The most obnoxious high school pitcher I've ever faced. It's a long story. I'll tell you some other time. I have to get going."

"You sure you don't wanna get high?" Pitts asked.

"Yeah."

I hopped down off the table and headed for my car, but stopped. Pitts was loading a little brown pipe.

"Hey," I said.

"Hey what?"

"I'll call you."

"Yeah, sure."

"Hey, Pitts," I said. "I've known it for a long time."

He looked up from his pipe. "Known what?"

"You aren't a loser. And that's a lot of bull about the Japs and robots."

"Think so?"

"Pretty soon you'll be learning how to make video games."

Pitts didn't say anything. I went on to my car and got in. As I drove away, I saw him sitting on the picnic table, holding a match to his pipe.

Ten

AS I DROVE OUT of the Hamilton Park neighborhood toward Nimbus Creek, I remembered that I had stayed up all night. My eyes were tired and my thoughts were a little jumbled, but I had no problem remembering Bean.

Jonathan Livingston Bean. Why would he be asking about me? Why would he want to see me? What could he possibly have to say to me?

I hadn't seen or heard of him for almost four years. Not since I had faced him when I was a ninth-grader and he was a senior.

That had been our first and last meeting. I was fourteen years old. It was the year I was brought up from the ninth grade to the varsity high school baseball team.

It was only the third game of the season, and only my

third game on the varsity squad. We were playing a school in our division called Stanton. It was a night game and we were playing at home on Nimbus Creek Field. There wasn't a trace of wind. Not a trace.

I wasn't pitching that day; I was playing first base and batting number 6 in the lineup. Bean was on the mound for Stanton, and he was awesome. For the first eight innings he had a two-hitter going, with nine strikeouts. He'd struck me out twice, and both times he'd made me look like a fool.

Bean was cocky, arrogant, and obnoxious. Whenever he struck out a batter, he would lick his index finger and make a big imaginary chalk mark in the air. He had a floozy blond girlfriend who looked like she should have been posing in a bikini beside a souped-up Chevy in *Hot Rod* magazine. Before every inning, before going out to the mound to take his warm-up pitches, Bean would meet his girl at the chain-link fence and they'd stick their lips through one of the openings and smack loudly.

There was a story circulating about Bean. Few people knew it, but somehow I had picked it up.

The story was that Bean carried in his back pocket a sharp object which he used for doctoring the baseball. He would make certain gouges or notches on the baseball, and then throw a pitch that was supposedly unhittable.

This alleged pitch had been dubbed the Beanerball. People said he resorted to this Beanerball only once or twice a game, in crucial situations.

But there was no proof that it even existed, only hearsay, passed along from one person to another. To me, it sounded like the kind of tale one of his many enemies would invent. Nobody could agree exactly how he gouged the baseball. Some people said he used half a staple remover; others said a paperclip, a bottle cap, thumbtack, custom-made ring (as Whitey Ford had done), a nail file, his girlfriend's wisdom tooth, et cetera.

So that evening three and a half years ago, when I saw the legendary Bean for the first time, I watched him carefully. Being a pitcher myself, I could pretty much tell when he was throwing a fastball, a curve, or a slider, and he was throwing them all well. As I said, he had struck me out both times I'd come to bat and had made me look pretty silly.

By the bottom of the ninth, we were behind 3–0, but we had managed to load the bases. There were two outs. And guess who was at bat.

There I was, a mere ninth-grader, only my third game of the season, stepping up to the plate. Bean grinned at me from the mound and all but blew me a kiss. He went into his stretch, checked the runner on third, and delivered a fastball—right at my head. I ducked, dropped the bat, sprawled to the dirt.

When I got up, trembling and quivering all over, I started walking out to the mound, straight for Bean, intending to kill him. Bean dropped his mitt and waved me toward him with both hands, a big smirk on his face. Somebody—it must have been our third-base coach—grabbed me around the waist from behind and held me. At the same time, both of our benches unloaded and the guys were sort of milling around out by pitcher's mound, no punches being thrown.

Coach Agbar was screaming into the ump's face that Bean should be ejected for throwing at my head. Bean put his palms up in a "Who *me*?" gesture. Both teams continued to stand around. Amazingly, the ump took all of Coach Agbar's abuse. He must have known Agbar was right, but he didn't have the guts to eject Bean from the game.

Eventually, things settled down and the teams returned to their dugouts. I was back in the batter's box, knocking the dust from my cleats with my bat.

Bean whizzed the next two fastballs right by me for strikes. The count was 1 and 2.

As I said, I had been studying Bean's every move the whole game, and now I saw him make a few quick movements with the ball in his glove that he hadn't made before. He was doing something to the ball inside his glove, but like a magician, he was also creating a distraction by making a big show of smoothing the dirt on the mound with his feet. At that moment, I became a believer: there *was* such a thing as a Beanerball, and Bean was about to throw it.

I called time and stepped out of the batter's box. Not wanting Bean to suspect that I knew something was fishy, I pretended to adjust my batting glove. What I was really doing was trying to think.

I had two choices. I could simply turn to the ump and ask him to check the ball. If Bean had doctored it, the ump would see it and eject Bean, and possibly Bean's team would have to forfeit the game.

Or I could step back into the batter's box and take my shot, with the slight advantage of knowing that Bean was about to throw a legendary pitch.

I stepped back up to the plate. I wanted to see that pitch with my own eyes.

Bean shook off two signs from the catcher, then nodded. This was all an act: Bean knew what he was going to throw, and he must have had a way of signaling it to his catcher.

Bean started his motion to the plate. The Beanerball was on its way.

I was not disappointed by that pitch. I will never forget it as long as I live. The ball actually seemed to wobble its way toward my head. But this time I didn't duck. I waited and hung in there, and sure enough, it dropped into the strike zone. As it did, I took a stride into the ball, my hands came around with the speed of light, my body uncoiled, my wrists snapped, and I felt the bat connect—the *zing* go through my hands, down to my feet—the *crack*, the ball jumping off the bat, rising and rising, sailing over the right-field home-run wall, still rising, past the tall towers of lights, up and over the big grassy hill, and out of sight into the darkness. A grand slam. We won the game 4–3.

As I trotted around the bases, I didn't even glance at Bean.

I was looking to where the ball had gone. Looking with absolute astonishment. I could hardly believe my eyes. The ball had cleared the second fence that ran along the ridge of the hill, a distance of 507 feet from home plate.

That started the controversy. For the next day or two, there was discussion about what had actually happened to that home-run ball when it left my bat. There was of course no question that it had cleared the *first* wall for a home run. But the question was whether it could possibly have cleared that second chain-link fence along the ridge of the hill. Since there were no lights up there, the ball had pretty much disappeared into the darkness.

Fortunately, it turned out that seven people had been standing out by the wall in right field, and they all claimed they thought *maybe* the ball had cleared the second fence.

The trouble was, Mickey Mantle, Hank Aaron, Babe Ruth, and their colleagues had hit few if any 507-foot home runs during their lifetime. People were understandably a little skeptical that a fourteen-year-old freshman had hit a ball that far on a windless evening. And before long, the seven people who had said they saw the ball *maybe* go over the fence now said, Well, no, it hadn't actually *cleared* the second fence, it had bounced against the side of the hill and rolled back down part of the way, and some kid had snatched it and run off with it. One of them said it was a girl with glasses; another said it was a frizzy-haired boy; and then two or three more said it was a frizzy-haired boy—and, yeah, that's what it was, all right, a frizzy-haired boy had run halfway up the hillside, scooped up the baseball, and run off with it.

And a few days later they actually produced a real live frizzy-haired kid, who produced a real live baseball and asked me to sign it, "To Ed, from your friend Dean Duffy."

I refused to sign the ball. During all the hubbub, I had pretty much kept quiet. I knew what I had seen, and that was that. The ball had gone over the second fence. I didn't make a big deal out of it; I let people argue, and I stayed out of it. But I refused to sign old Ed's baseball, because I knew it wasn't the ball *I* had hit. It was a fake. It didn't have a single mark on it, and I knew the one Bean had thrown me was doctored up.

It would have had gouges or notches or something in it. And besides, I knew it couldn't be the ball, because the ball I'd hit had cleared the second fence and gone into the ravine below. There was a steep 200-foot drop on the other side of the fence. That ball was lost forever.

Word went around that Dean Duffy wouldn't sign a frizzy-haired kid's grand-slam souvenir. What a snob. What a prima donna.

Then, soon enough, everybody forgot about the whole thing.

It didn't really make me angry that no one believed me. Even Jack Trant—who'd had to leave the game early that night and hadn't seen me hit the home run—even Jack had to admit that he found it very, very hard to believe the ball had gone that far.

I didn't really have time to be angry with anybody. I was a fourteen-year-old playing with and against eighteen-year-olds, and I had to stay focused on the here and now. But I never stopped believing that the Beanerball had cleared the second fence that night. Did it make any difference whether or not the ball had gone over? Absolutely. It was simply the difference between doing something great and doing something immortal.

Later, at breakfast, I told Jack and Shilo all about my first night, including my conversation with Pitts. I asked Jack if he remembered J. L. Bean.

"Sure, I remember Bean. How could I not remember the pitcher you hit your first high school grand salami off of? I only wish I hadn't missed seeing it. But I'd actually heard of our friend Bean before that. He'd had phenomenal sophomore and junior years. The colleges were all recruiting him and the pros were scouting him, but nobody liked his attitude. He had one lousy hunk of attitude."

"Did he end up getting any offers?" I asked.

"Naw. He fizzled out his senior year. Faded right into oblivion. That doesn't take anything away from the grand slam you hit off him that night, though. I was there for the first seven innings and Bean was awful tough that night. But no, he just didn't do anything his senior year. Who knows," Jack added jokingly, "maybe it was your grand slam that did it to him."

"Did what?"

"Shook him up. Rattled his confidence. I've seen it happen. Especially those cocky ones like Bean. They give up a couple of long balls and they lose heart. They get overcautious. Could be old Bean is holding a big-time grudge against you. Maybe that's why he's looking for you. You'd better watch it."

"Watch it?" I said. "I don't follow you."

"Well," Jack said, "maybe he figures he's got a score to settle with you."

We also talked about the part-time job. When Jack described it, I couldn't wait to get started on Monday. It sounded perfect, the ideal part-time job. Jack had come through again, and, as usual, all I could do was thank him, even though I wished I could do more.

All during breakfast, Shilo kept giving me these long, searching looks. I could tell something was on her mind, and finally she came out with it.

"Dean, I don't like this staying up all night. I want you to take care of yourself. I mean it."

"All right," I said.

"In fact," she said, "when you're finished here I think you should go back to the apartment and get some sleep."

Actually, that sounded like a pretty good idea.

Eleven

BACK AT THE APARTMENT, I took a long nap, and when I woke up, I found that I had a mighty craving for baked beans. Maybe it meant I subconsciously wanted J. L. Bean, although this struck me as silly. I rummaged through a cupboard and to my delight found a can of my favorite brand of beans hiding way in the back behind a box of Rice-A-Roni. I opened the can the old-fashioned way—non-electrically—and began shoveling the cool beans from the can to my mouth at a steady rhythm, not bothering to sit down. This made me feel like I was "roughing it."

After I finished, I stared contentedly out the kitchen window at the rain. Then, for the next half hour, I made an honest attempt to water Ned's plants according to his directions.

At some point I remembered Ruta Waterfall and the ticket Rose had left me. Maybe I'd at least go and have a look.

On my way to the Wallingford District, I stopped at an automatic teller machine and replenished my wallet. The part-time job I was starting on Monday would help, but I knew I'd have to be careful this fall about withdrawing money from my savings account whenever I felt like it.

At eight minutes to 8 p.m., I circled the block where the Annie Greenday Bookstore was located, wondering once more how and why a woman named Ruta could possibly do anything of interest in a bookstore named Annie. At four minutes to eight I scored a rather nice but oily parking spot on a side street. With freshly scented armpits and a clean white T-shirt, I strolled through the mild rain to the bookstore.

Plenty of people were arriving. On the door was the Ruta flyer, stamped SOLD OUT. Praise be, a scalper's delight.

I positioned myself near the door, making eye contact with some of the arrivees, as if to communicate to them that I had a ticket I wanted to get rid of for as much money as they'd be sucker enough to give me. But I felt too much like a drug dealer or a beggar, and I had to admit I was sort of curious. So I went inside.

Fifteen or twenty people were browsing through stacks of books. I noticed a smiling woman taking tickets from a line of people filing through a doorway. I tried to see where they were going, but I couldn't see much. Here was the moment of decision: either get up the gumption and start peddling my ticket, or get up even more gumption and use it.

Well, I was looking for something this fall, wasn't I? For answers? Experiences? All right, Duffy, start looking.

Handing my ticket to the woman in the doorway, I entered a big living room or lounge, about the size of a regulation basketball court. This room was furnished with chairs, tables, lamps, sofas, and wall hangings. At the far end of the room was a small elevated stage. To one side of the stage was a piano in front of a fireless fireplace. The room was crowded with people mingling and chatting, maybe two hundred people, a good three-fourths of them middle-aged women.

Many were drinking tea from Styrofoam cups. Tea. I've never quite known why the smell of it always produces a sort of foul, menacing mood in me, similar to what disco music and Happy Faces have done to many people before me.

I found the source of the Styrofoam cups: a long table set against one wall of the room, with big silver insulated beverage dispensers the size of kegs. Help yourself. I searched for coffee, but found only tea and hot cider. I poured some of the hot cider into a Styrofoam cup and took a sip. It tasted like tea.

Just then a woman who seemed to be in charge of the whole thing stepped up onto the stage. She burst into smiles and waves as she spotted various individuals she knew, then raised her hands for silence. Then she saw more people she knew and smiled and gave them eager waves, at last resuming her quieting-down posture.

"Please, everyone, please. May I have your attention." There was no microphone, but she didn't really need one. She had an outdoorsy, twangy voice, like a

camp counselor or a PE teacher. "We want everyone—
we want everyone to be able to see, so maybe the people toward the front can kind of sit down on the carpet.
Or—" she waved her hands, and her sleeves flapped—
"*arrange* yourselves any way you can!"

There was a good deal of laughter as people maneu-
vered for position. I walked around the room, trying not
to touch anyone. (It's a game I play in crowds.) I took a
position toward the back, near the exit. I tried another
sip of the cider, then put the cup down beside me on
the floor.

"Okay, well, good evening everybody," the woman
said. "I'm T. J. Lukens, for those of you who don't know
me, and welcome to Annie Greenday Bookstore, and an
evening with Ruta Waterfall."

During the introduction, I spotted the most likely
candidate for Ruta Waterfall, standing offstage. She was
holding a large black suitcase. What was in there? Magic
tricks? A juggling act? A small child? She was tall and
hefty, what my mom called "a husky gal." Not fat, but
definitely pear-shaped. Her hair was gray-streaked and
flowing over her shoulders. Her smile was placid.

Why was I here?

Why was I occupying an apartment in the University
District until December 20? Why wasn't I in college,
camped out in a library, studying my brains out? Why
wasn't I working, earning a living, paying rent for an
apartment of my own? Why was I alone? Where were
all my friends? Why wasn't I on a date, courting a girl
I really cared about? Why hadn't I joined the army? Or
the merchant marine? Good God, I was about to turn
eighteen, the age for going off to war or to sea. Not for

standing in a room with a bunch of middle-aged women.

When T. J. Lukens finished her introduction, Ruta Waterfall stepped forward and the two women hugged. Then T. J. Lukens left the stage and cut through the middle of the crowd, heading directly for me. She passed right by me—almost touched me with her sleeve. I saw her face as she passed—no makeup, a network of tiny wrinkles around her eyes and mouth, three or four long blond hairs growing out of her chin. She stood behind me and in front of the exit, as if to block it. Apparently, she was going to nab anyone who tried to make a getaway.

Ruta Waterfall started talking, but I wasn't quite finished staring at T. J. Lukens. Her earrings . . . they were huge round objects . . . like sand dollars. My God, they *were* sand dollars. I shuddered.

Ruta Waterfall had a high, tremulous voice and could not say her *s*'s; the *s* sound came out as a chirping whistle.

". . . pleasure to be here . . . don't often get to . . . special privilege . . . my good friend T. J. . . ."

She opened her suitcase and withdrew a flute. My heart sank. She shook her long grayish hair out of her face and went through some strange contortions of mouth and tongue. When she introduced her first song, it sounded like "Peeing in Hell."

A woman standing next to me turned and said, "Excuse me, but I didn't catch that title. What song did she say?"

" 'Peeing in Hell,' " I said.

She gave me a dirty look.

Another woman in front of us, who must have overheard us, turned around. " 'Being, Inhale,' " she said to the woman, ignoring me. "It's called 'Being, Inhale.' It has to do with Mother Earth breathing life into the soul."

Ruta Waterfall's being inhaled and then exhaled and tweeted life into the flute. It was a jazzy number, as flute music goes, not much melody but a tempo you could snap your fingers to. A bearded man with a pony-tail joined in on the piano. People in the audience "re-sponded" to the music. Ruta Waterfall danced and trilled and tweeted. She turned in a circle one way. So did the audience. She turned in a circle the other way. So did the audience. She turned in several circles. Her hair flew.

Then she lowered the flute and started singing in a voice that was high and warbly, like a police siren under water. She sang:

> *Don't be scared!*
> *O-la-la*
> *Allow yourself to be dared!*
> *You won't fail,*
> *Hoo-lay-lay*
> *Let it all in,*
> *Being, inhale!*

I eyed the door.

She sang and she twirled, closed her eyes, swung her hair, glided, juked, boogied, bunny-hopped. The audi-ence swayed, rocked, writhed, and a few looked like they were getting goosed.

I was singing my own song. Flee, flee, flee! I calcu-lated the number of seconds it would take me to get to the door, knock down T. J. Lukens, sprint through the bookstore and out of the front door, into the Wallingford street.

> *Don't be timid*
> *Don't be scared*
> *Don't be afraid*
> *To dance la-la!*

She jumped off the stage and started dancing with members of the audience as the piano kept up the jazzy tempo. She nabbed a little man with bright orange hair and an orange, neatly styled beard and a black turtleneck sweater. He looked like a black-and-orange leprechaun.

> *Open your mouth*
> *Take a dee-heep breath*
> *Allow yourself*
> *To LIVE la-la*

The song ended. The crowd burst into applause.

The woman standing next to me who'd asked me the name of the song gave me sort of a smug smile as she applauded. I looked down at her feet. She was standing in what appeared to be a puddle of urine. I realized she had accidentally kicked over my Styrofoam cup.

Ruta Waterfall played on. The audience drew tighter together, closer to the stage, and with each song I felt myself becoming more a part of both the music and the audience.

Toward the end of the concert, without the piano,

Ruta played a slow, haunting melody on her flute. The hairs on the back of my neck prickled. The mournful tones seemed to go through me. A dampness welled up in my eyes.

Then Ruta removed the flute from her mouth and sang, unaccompanied. I closed my eyes and tears rolled down my face.

I was remembering that night in Lompoc when I had stood alone on a back-yard deck, hearing the wind swooshing the trees, the sound that had always made me feel vaguely uneasy. Who had I been that night and what had I accomplished and what did it mean? Who was I now, three years later? In my mind I could almost hear the sound of the wind in the trees, mingled with Ruta's voice, and they were speaking right to my soul. Thoughts and feelings were rising up in me. Fear, loneliness, love . . . What was I looking for? I was willing to look for anything, even if I didn't know what it was. I wanted a shot at something.

The song faded away. No one applauded; there was not a sound. Ruta lowered her flute, lowered her head. A few people near me were weeping. All were standing still, looking up at Ruta, whose head was still bowed.

Then there were rustling noises as people turned to each other and hugged. I felt a light touch on my arm. I turned and saw T. J. Lukens smiling at me. Her arms opened and she drew me into her, and I felt very homesick.

I left the Annie Greenday Bookstore shortly after that. I hurried to my car without speaking to anyone. I was confused and slightly embarrassed, but I was also elated.

What had happened to me in there? Whatever it was, I had the feeling that it was monumental. As if I had connected with myself in a way that I never had before.

What a day! What a beginning. Was my whole apartment-sitting gig going to be like this? Filled with new experiences and with powerful, intense feelings?

I felt exhilarated. What should I do? Where could I go? I wanted to be around people.

I ended up at the Hasty Tasty. My second night in a row.

I was glad to see the Hasty Tasty girl sitting on the stool, her knees clamped together, same jeans and same book as last night. I was content to stand at the counter and watch her read, but eventually she looked up, that pale beautiful face with the dark semicircles under the eyes.

"You again," she said.

"What, you haven't been fired yet?"

I knelt down and looked inside the dessert case. Same black cat, curled up in kitty fetal position.

I straightened up. "Give me an espresso."

She almost smiled.

I grabbed the last old-fashioned glazed doughnut from the tray and took it to the same table I'd sat at the night before.

The place was crowded and noisy. The majority of people were alone, most of them reading, highlighting passages in their textbooks with markers.

The Hasty Tasty girl brought me my espresso. Then she sat down at my table and lit a cigarette.

"If you're not a student," she asked, "what are you? What do you do?"

"Play golf," I said. It was the first thing that came into my mind, and seemed adequate.

"What, for a living?"

"No."

I poured packets of sugar into my espresso, stirred it, and tasted it. It was very bitter, and I forced myself not to grimace. Last night had been no mistake: the stuff was supposed to taste like this. The girl watched me, smoke trailing from her nostrils.

"How about you?" I asked. "You in or out of high school?"

"Oh, out."

She said it with irony, as if there were a story behind it.

"Graduated?" I asked.

She glanced over her shoulder. A student had come in from the rain and had been standing at the counter for a minute or so, looking all around for service, drenched and impatient. He was wearing a backpack that could be full of nothing but accounting or business textbooks.

The Hasty Tasty girl turned back to me. "What?"

"Graduated?"

"No, not exactly."

"Not exactly?"

"No, I just said screw it," she said.

"To school? You said screw it to high school?"

Once again she turned and looked at the wet student with the backpack. Suddenly he slapped the counter once. *Splat.* Wow. You had to hand it to the guy; it takes some nerve to slap a counter. The fat dishwasher emerged from the kitchen, looking curious and holding a half-eaten glazed old-fashioned doughnut up to his mouth, chewing slowly, gazing blandly at the student.

"Um, what?" she said, turning back to me.

"You said screw it?"

She nodded.

"How come?"

"Long story. I'll have to give you the short version. One day, spring of my junior year, the principal calls me into his office and says, You can't go on the field trip to Snoqualmie Falls. Why not? Because you have too many unexcused absences and you're lacking in this credit and that credit and if you don't go to summer school you'll have to repeat junior year. So I said screw you and this place. Screw it all. I got the heck out of there."

I could picture it. She was as confused and mixed up as the rest of us, and she might say screw it to some things, but I was pretty sure she didn't have an ounce of quit in her.

"That was last spring?" I said.

"Spring before last."

"You're not going back?"

"Nope."

"Why did you have so many absences?"

She hesitated, and smiled. "That's the long version."

"Which you probably don't go telling to any joker who walks in off the street," I said.

She stood up to leave, even though the guy with the backpack had stomped out a minute ago, and said, "Some other time, joker."

Twelve

MONDAY MORNING I drove out to the part-
time job. My destination was a construction site somewhere near Brier, one of those rural areas outside of
Seattle that had been chomped by developers.

I turned off the main road onto a smaller road, then
onto a still smaller one, and finally up a long, steep,
muddy driveway where I could reach out and give high-
fives to the outstretched twigs. After about a half mile,
I came to a clearing at the top of the hill. Here was the
site. It was surrounded on three sides by thick woods,
but the fourth side opened to a stunning view of the
valley.

In the middle of the lot was a mountain of rubble
about the size of a two-story house, which was exactly
what it had once been. According to Jack, the four kids
had all grown up and moved away, and the retired par-

94

ents had sold the property and bought an RV. The buyer had hired Jack's firm to tear down the old house and build a brand-new modern one. Jack's crew had done the tearing down but weren't to start construction until late spring, after the building permit came through and the architect's plans were finished.

My job was to haul the old house, load by load, to the dump.

I had the use of a green Chevy pickup, which Jack had instructed his crew to leave parked at the site, along with a wheelbarrow and a long plank to use as a ramp. I would leave the pickup parked at the site when I wasn't hauling loads of rubble to the dump. Jack would pay me by the load, verifiable by the dump receipts I was to turn in every Friday afternoon to his secretary. I'd work entirely on my own, whatever hours I chose.

I spent some time walking around the heap of rubble, surveying it from all sides. It had scraps and debris, old doors and windows, miscellaneous household junk, even some busted furniture—the remains of a home and a family that had lived there for years.

I started the truck and revved it, just to see what kind of shape it was in. Not bad for an old clunker. I backed it right up against the mountain of rubble and shut the motor off. I found a pair of work gloves under the seat and put them on.

I got out and went around back and lowered the tailgate. Then I started grabbing things and throwing them into the bed of the truck.

Each day that week I made two and sometimes three trips to the dump. When I had a full load, I'd cover it with a tarp, lash the four corners to the sides of the truck, and lay the plank across it to keep the tarp from billowing on the highway. I drove carefully down the rut-filled driveway. Out on the road, with a twenty-two-mile drive to the dump, I found that it was a whole new experience driving a truck instead of a beat-up '63 Volvo. Other motorists seemed to respect my truck and my load and the sign on my door that read TRANT CON-STRUCTION. Truck drivers and other working people would often nod at me, and I'd nod back at them.

The dump was a great place. I'd wait in line to be waved in by the worker, and I'd back my truck into the stall, right up to the edge of the pit. People on either side of me would be busy dumping their loads. Standing on top of my own load, I'd fling and hurl it piece by piece into the pit, where every few minutes a monster bulldozer would come along and shove all the garbage up to the crusher.

Breakable objects that crashed and shattered and splintered were especially satisfying. Windows and mirrors were frosting on the cake.

I loved the job. Each morning I woke up excited to drive out to Brier amid the bursting fall colors, to my mountain of rubble.

In a way, it was a lot like the work I'd done all summer on San Juan Island. There was nothing to think about or worry about or plan—I just did what I had to do. I had a clear, simple purpose. And it crossed my mind more than once that week that maybe this job, or one like it, was my future.

But I didn't do only physical labor that first full week of apartment sitting. When I wasn't at the rubble heap, I was usually sitting at Ned and Rose's desk, pulling my hair out, completing that Shute application. I hashed out my answers to the essay questions on sheets of notebook paper, then typed them up on Ned and Rose's personal computer and printed them. Sometimes I felt as though I were pouring my heart out, and other times I said to myself, "Oh, the hell with it; just tell them whatever they want to hear."

On Friday, my eighth day in the apartment, I finished the application and sent it off. If I got accepted, I'd have until December 13 to sign the letter of intent, which was the equivalent of accepting money for one semester's tuition, room, and board. It occurred to me, while I stood in line at the post office with my big manila envelope, that maybe I'd done such a lousy job on the application that no amount of clout by Drago or Jack would get me accepted to Shute. In a way, that would be a relief. It was relief enough to be rid of the application.

A few days after sending off the application, I started sitting in on some of the big lecture classes at the UW, where there was no way anyone could know whether or not I was really a student. My favorite was "Decline of Western Thought," taught by a crusty old professor whose books my mom had read. The class met three mornings a week, two hundred people in a lecture theater big enough to hold twice that number. I always sat in the same seat in the very last row. Only one other guy sat back there, so we both had plenty of space to stretch out and put our feet up.

That other guy always wore the same purple UW warm-up jacket and baseball hat, and never took them off. A long tuft of his hair stuck up through the back of his cap. He had a pimply, but not hideous, complexion. He would try to take notes for the first five minutes of the lecture, but he'd always end up falling sound asleep.

He was a baseball player.

I knew this from the first moment I saw him, even though I had never seen him before. It wasn't his warm-up jacket and hat; I would have known even if he hadn't worn those. I felt an immediate kinship with him. I wanted to know who he was and where he came from. I even wanted to be his friend. Who knows, maybe I had played against him and subconsciously remembered him. I don't know why he intrigued me so much, but I was positive that one of these days I would introduce myself to this fellow left-hander.

Those rainy mild October days fell into their own routine and rhythm. I was happy. I would never be this free again.

But I had spells of loneliness and homesickness, too. I was all right during the day, but at night I needed to be around people. So I usually camped out in the undergraduate library. I read and read; I spent hours with the other students, the real ones, studying, outlining, summarizing. I attacked books the same way I had attacked the mountain of rubble and the house on San Juan Island. I used Ned's student card to check out books and take them back to the apartment. But I preferred camping out in the library. I would often stay till ten or eleven. Then I'd take a couple of books and walk back to the apartment or, more likely, to the Hasty Tasty.

The Hasty Tasty girl was usually there, and she'd fix me an espresso without my having to order it. I'd grab a doughnut, sit down at a table by the window, and open one of my books. Often she'd sit down with me to smoke a cigarette. We didn't talk much, didn't even know each other's names. I liked thinking of her as the Hasty Tasty girl, and I wondered if she had a name for me. I liked not having to tell who I was.

"Are you rich?" she asked me one night. "Do you have a rich daddy or something? You seem to lead this life of leisure. You're not a student, right? Yet you hang around like one."

"I work the same way you work here," I said. "When I feel like it."

She ignored my joke. "I thought you said you play golf."

"In the spring I do," I said. "It's not spring yet."

"You're waiting for spring? I knew you were waiting for something. You have that look. I guess everybody's waiting for something."

The more I saw her, the more I liked her. And the more I found myself thinking about her, and wondering what it would be like to know her outside of the Hasty Tasty. Once or twice, when she sat down at my table, I almost asked her out, but didn't. It wasn't so much a lack of nerve as . . . I wasn't sure what. That I was feeling like a transient. That everything seemed temporary and in transition. I was apartment sitting only until December 20. After that, I didn't know what I'd be doing or where I'd be. But I was sure that if there was anybody in Seattle I wanted to know better, the Hasty Tasty girl was the one.

Often my nights wouldn't end after the Hasty Tasty. I'd walk back to the apartment, hop into my car, and cruise the neighborhoods of Seattle. I loved driving through dark residential streets in the dead of night, passing parked cars instead of being passed by moving ones.

Invariably, I'd haunt some old baseball field that I had played on, but more often than not, I'd end up at Nimbus Creek Field, my home field, where I'd hit that monumental home run off of Bean. I'd walk around the deserted field, trying to imagine myself playing baseball again. Or not playing baseball again.

"I don't think you're getting enough sleep," Shilo said one day in early November. "You look pale."

"And how about exercise?" Jack said. "You keeping in shape? Lifting any weights?"

"I'm lifting plenty of rubble," I said. "That part-time job's keeping me in shape."

"I think you're eating too much junk food," Shilo said.

"I want you swinging a baseball bat," Jack said. "A weighted one. You still have your lead-weighted bat?"

"Yeah. In my trunk."

"Start swinging it."

"All right."

"You haven't run into old J. L. Bean yet, have you?" Jack asked.

"Not yet."

"You're not sleeping regularly," Shilo said. "And what's this?" She touched my face. "Stubble? You're not shaving these days?"

"I kind of like stubble," I said.

"Don't let yourself fall apart," Jack said. "Stay in shape. Aw, hell, what am I worrying about? You'll be in as good a shape as you need to be when the time comes."

The November days grew colder and shorter. Usually in the morning, after watering Ned's plants, I'd go for a run in Ravenna Park. Then I'd sit in on that "Decline of Western Thought" class and watch that baseball player nod off to sleep. I usually tried to do at least one load a day at the construction sight, but there was less and less daylight for outdoor work, and amazingly, that rubble heap didn't seem to be getting any smaller. Besides, it was pretty lonely way out there. Maybe the job wasn't as perfect as I thought.

Afternoons I would play pickup basketball at the intramural activities building, or read, or hit some baseballs at the automated batting cage. A couple of times I played golf with Jack. For dinner, when I didn't eat at the Trants', I'd cook something in the apartment or grab some fast food and eat it in my car.

Even though I was frequently around people, I started to feel more and more isolated. I craved more human contact. I called my folks often to check on the progress of Duffy Inn and to let them know how I was doing. I called Pitts a few times, but he was always either not home or sleeping, so I left my phone number with his mother. I thought more and more about taking a step forward with the Hasty Tasty girl and asking her out, or at least finding out her name, but so far I hadn't gotten past thinking about it.

And so the days went by slowly. There were times when I thought I was happy, that I was proving that I could be happy doing something besides baseball. I mean, I'd been reading books like never before, working hard at a good honest job, exploring the city, opening my eyes and ears to the world.

But there were other times when I wondered, Is this all there is? Where was the excitement and enthusiasm for life that I glimpsed at the Ruta Waterfall concert? Where was the thrill—the fireworks? The feeling of accomplishment, of reward and challenge? Of being tested and pushed to your limit?

And where was the soul-searching, the "looking within" that I was supposed to be doing? Almost six weeks had gone by since I moved into the apartment, and I wasn't one whit closer to knowing whether I'd ever play ball again.

Ten days before Thanksgiving, I got a call from Pitts. He said he had a few hours to kill before work. When I asked him how it was going, he said not bad, except for one minor thing.

"What minor thing?" I asked him.

"Man," he said, "I miss drugs."

"Ever had an espresso?" I asked.

"A what?"

An hour later he met me at the Hasty Tasty. It was only six o'clock and the Hasty Tasty girl wasn't on duty yet, which made it kind of strange for me to be there. It was even stranger sitting across a table from Pitts. Except that he was chain-smoking cigarettes, he appeared to be all right.

We talked a little. He told me that he was saving his money so he could move out of his parents' house into a place of his own. He was still going to take the training course at his work, but had found out that he wasn't eligible for it until spring. He was glad of that. "I think they make you take a drug test," he said. "I'd like to make sure I pass it."

A few days later it was Pitts's day off, and believe it or not, we played golf at a local city course. He had dug his old clubs out of the basement. It was a wet, blustery day, and except for a few hard-core golfers, we pretty much had the course to ourselves. We got cold and soaked and lost a lot of balls, but it wasn't as disappointing as it could have been.

After the game, as we were walking back to our cars in the parking lot, he turned to me. "Dean, what're you going to do with yourself?"

"I don't know yet."

"I'm no expert," he said, "but you still got one of the purest swings I've ever seen. Hey, did you ever meet up with that Bean guy?"

I shook my head. "I thought about tracking him down, but I'm not even sure how to find him. Or if I want to find him."

"You never did tell me the story behind him."

"I hit a grand slam off him once. A 507-foot grand slam."

"Oh, that one, huh?" Pitts said. "Yeah, I remember that."

"You do?"

"Sure. I remember there was a big argument about it in my math class. My math teacher spent about twenty minutes explaining why it was mathematically impossible for that baseball to clear the—"

"Yeah, I know, I know," I said. "But it *did* clear the outer fence. I know it did."

Pitts shrugged. "What difference does it make, anyway? It's not like it was the only thing you ever did. What's it got to do with anything?"

"That pitch of Bean's," I said, "he was throwing me a doctored ball. He'd done something to it. I could've told the ump and had Bean thrown out right on the spot. We would've won the game by forfeit."

"How do you know it was doctored?" Pitts asked. "You couldn't know that for sure."

"Oh, I knew. And you should've seen the way that ball danced when it came at me. I had to keep my head in there. Then it dropped—bam—right into the strike zone. I nailed it. It was one of the greatest moments of my life. That and the day we beat Cuba in Lompoc."

Pitts glanced at me.

We reached our cars, which were parked side by side, and stood between them.

"It's all history," he said. "I never did get much out of history."

"History . . . yeah, I suppose," I said. "But it was the longest ball I ever hit in my life. The longest I'll ever hit. I'll never feel that big again. Maybe I'm not a loser, but I'll never be that big a winner again."

"How do you know? Man, you can hope, can't you?"

"What do I base it on?" I said. "That I have a good golf swing?"

"Hell, Duffy," Pitts said, "you were a great hitter."

"I lost it."

"You can get it back."

"How? By hoping?"

"I don't know, man. By trying, I guess. The way you tried when Bean threw you the doctored baseball. You said it yourself, you didn't even have to step back into the batter's box. You could've called him on it right there. But you gambled and won."

"Sure, I was just a kid. I didn't know any better. I didn't have any fear. I know too much now, Pitts. And there's a whole lot more at stake that I'd be gambling on. There's a lot more to lose."

Pitts shrugged. He opened his car door and put his clubs in. "Sounds like you got your mind made up," he said.

The day after my golf game with Pitts, I left the library around eleven-thirty and went back to the apartment. I planned to have some scrambled eggs with cheese and then catch up on some sleep.

I picked up Ned and Rose's mail from the box in the lobby. There was a letter addressed to me from Dick Drago. I opened it.

You'll be getting a formal letter from the admissions office in a few days, but I thought I'd be the first to tell you. Congratulations, you've been accepted. Which means the next move is yours. I'll need a decision from you, one way or the other, no later than December 13, preferably earlier. I'll be in touch with you.

Drago

I phoned Jack as soon as I got upstairs. When he heard my news, he quickly forgave me for phoning at midnight.

I was no longer in the mood for scrambled eggs or sleep. A little human contact seemed called for. It was high time I did something daring. I made up my mind: I was going to ask the Hasty Tasty girl for a date.

I stuffed Drago's letter into my back pocket and headed for the Hasty Tasty.

Thirteen

THE HASTY TASTY was jammed with its usual assortment of oddballs who were having conversations with one another or with the furniture, playing chess or watching it being played, reading a book or one of the newspapers from the rack, staring at something or at nothing.

Wanting to get there as soon as I could, I had driven my car instead of walking. Fortunately, the Hasty Tasty girl was working tonight. She brought me my little black espresso, but she didn't sit down at my table just then. That was all right. It gave me time to muster my courage.

Five minutes later, she emerged from behind the counter. She was holding a pack of cigarettes and a dishrag but wasn't using either. As she passed the scraggly bearded guy I was used to seeing here, he reached out and touched her arm but said nothing. She gave him a cigarette and then a light. He didn't acknowledge this. I watched her move around the Hasty Tasty, picking up a stray cup and saucer, wiping an occasional table, stopping to talk to someone or look at one of the newspapers. Everything she did seemed natural and graceful and slightly bored, not a bit self-conscious. I wanted very much for her to come over and say hi, and a minute or two later she did.

"Hi."

"Hi."

"How's your espresso?"

"Fine."

"No doughnut for you tonight?"

"No. You busy?"

"No." She sat down and took out a cigarette.

"Who is that guy?" I asked, nodding toward the scragbeard.

"Don."

I guess she figured that said it all. She lit her cigarette. I drank my espresso and looked at the girl, and could not find anything not beautiful about her. I didn't think there could be such a thing as a perfect nose, but she had one. The only features I couldn't see were her ears, because her dark thick hair covered them, and her neck. I could see her smooth throat, though, and her collarbone. She didn't seem to be wearing any makeup, and her complexion was somewhat pale in spite of its Hasty Tasty hue.

"He once accused me of calling him a mutt," I said.

"Don?"

"Yeah."

"Did you?"

"No."

"He's come in almost every night since I started working here," she said.

"When was that?"

"That I started here? Oh, last April or June or something."

"What do you know about him?"

"About as much as I know about you," she said. "Actually, I know more about him. I know his name."

I promptly told her mine. "Now Don and I are back on equal ground," I said.

"You're ahead," she said. "I don't know his last name."

"What's your name?" I asked.

She told me.

"Maybe we're friends now," I said.

"That's not so bad," she said.

"No," I said.

I felt encouraged and happy. I felt so happy I almost laughed. "I-uh—" I felt myself grinning. "Maybe if you—we could—" I stopped. Whatever words I'd been rehearsing were useless.

She stubbed her cigarette out in the glass ashtray and blew smoke into the air indifferently.

We were silent. She neither got up to leave nor lit another cigarette.

"Do you like art?" she finally asked.

"Art?"

"Yeah."

"Paintings and sculptures and that?"

"Yes," she said. "Do you like it?"

"No," I said.

Then it slowly dawned on me that she might have a

motive for asking me about art. "I don't dislike it," I said.

"You're neutral," she said.

"No, I wouldn't say neutral," I said.

"Sounds neutral to me," she said.

"All right," I said. "I'll say I'm neutral."

"That's dandy," she said. She began wiping the table with the dishrag. "That's a dandy conversation," she said to the dishrag.

"It's my fault," I said. "Do you know a good place to—a good gallery?"

"For what?" she asked.

"Viewing art," I said.

"With you?"

"Yes."

"That's more or less what I was aiming at a minute ago," she said lightly.

"Yes, well," I said, once again very happy, "let's do it. When do you sleep?"

"What?"

"What hours do you sleep?"

"I go to bed when I get home from work and I get up around eleven in the morning."

No wonder she looked so tired all the time. "We could go tomorrow in the afternoon," I said.

She stood up. She had to go back to the counter to wait on a middle-aged man and woman. This gave me time to take a few breaths. I gulped the rest of my espresso and wiped the corners of my mouth with a napkin.

She returned a few minutes later. "Tomorrow afternoon would be fine," she said.

"Shall I pick you up?" I asked.

"Let's meet there," she said.

"All right," I said.

She did not sit down but stayed at the table for a minute.

"Is two o'clock all right?" I asked.

She nodded.

"Two it is, then," I said. I raised my empty cup and took a sip of nothing. I put it back down.

She had to leave again, but came back to pick up my cup and saucer.

"Oh, by the way," I said, "I don't think I caught where we're meeting."

"Oh!" she said.

Then she did something very strange. Something that made me like her even more than I had five minutes ago. She put down my cup and saucer, took a tiny pencil from her pocket, and wrote something on a napkin. The pencil was no longer than my pinky. She slid the napkin across the table to me. I looked from her brown eyes to the faint gray letters on the napkin. What she had written was unreadable. But I squinted and tried anyway. "Thalgy? Hippew?"

"Hughes," she said firmly, putting her hand on the napkin and rotating it slightly. "The Hughes Gallery."

"The one right on campus?"

"You know it?"

"Yes," I said. "Why didn't you just say it?"

"I felt like writing it." She started to pull the napkin toward her, but I snatched it and stuffed it in my pocket on top of Dick Drago's note.

"For my scrapbook," I said.

She smiled, slowly shaking her head, and started back toward the counter.

Fourteen

THE NEXT DAY I walked in the drizzle to the Hughes Gallery. The campus seemed strangely deserted. The sky was dark and everything was wet, but the air wasn't cold for mid-November, and I was comfortable in only a gray hooded sweatshirt over a T-shirt.

I reached the Hughes and walked into the foyer. The wet rubber of my tennis shoes squeaked on the linoleum floor. The high-ceilinged foyer was empty and poorly lighted. On my right was the gift shop, where a college girl sat behind the counter reading a textbook. Straight ahead was the entrance to the gallery, guarded by a skinny guy dressed in black, sitting primly behind a table, writing. When I approached, squeaking, he paused from his writing and looked up at me, annoyed and squinting behind his glasses, obviously trying to decide whether I was worth acknowledging. He decided I wasn't and promptly resumed his scribbling.

Standing still, I looked all around. The only sound I heard was the scratching of the guy's pen.

She wasn't there yet. I walked back through the foyer and outside. I'd wait for her under the front awning. Which direction would she approach from? Would she walk, drive, or take a bus from her house—or apartment? Who was she? I probably would know the answer to these questions, except for the last one, by the end of the day.

It was after two. Had we said three? Hardly anyone passed by. Those who did had umbrellas and looked intent on being somewhere else. They didn't even glance at the Hughes Gallery.

Heck, it only cost a dollar for students. (I checked inside my wallet to make sure I'd brought Ned's student card.) You'd think one or two of these students might pop into the gallery on a dark November afternoon. Why the hurry?

The sign that announced the current exhibit read, "Northwest Prospectus: Visions of Our Region by Sixteen Pacific Northwest Artists." Well, maybe it didn't exactly grab you by the hair and pull you inside, but as art themes went, it could have been worse.

The wind picked up and blew against my damp sweatshirt. The sky grew darker. I admitted I was cold. The Hasty Tasty girl—Karin—was late. I said her name aloud: "Karin." She pronounced the first syllable "car." I liked that. I stood there shivering, liking her name.

Then she appeared. She came from the direction of the Ave. She was wearing a light blue reversible waterproof jacket. The yellow hood was down. Her brown shoes would not have been considered practical by a parent. No umbrella—good for her. Her almost-damp hair blew behind her.

I forgot about being cold.

She apologized for being late but didn't offer a reason. We stood under the awning for a minute, not saying anything, looking at the sign I had read a few minutes ago. Her face was flushed from cold and exercise. She looked very healthy in a small-town high school way, about as un-Hasty Tasty as you could get.

"Did you walk from where you live?" I asked.

"No, I took the bus. I don't have a car."

"Where do you live?"

"Wallingford."

"Anywhere near the Annie Greenday Bookstore?"

She smiled, slightly surprised. "Three blocks south. Have you been there?"

"Once."

We went into the foyer. Again my shoes squelched and squeaked on the floor. The guy at the table was still writing.

Karin took care of her own ticket, despite my offer. She paid the full non-student price, which the guy fussily tucked into a metal box.

I flashed him Ned's student card and plunked down a buck.

"Um, excuse me," he said, folding his hands. "May I see that card again?"

"You may," I said.

He looked busily from the card to my face. "That isn't you," he said.

I laughed. I had used Ned's card fifty times and no

one else had even looked at the picture, let alone cared whose it was.

"I'm sorry," he said, shaking his head, "but that is *not* you."

"I never said it was," I said, and walked past him into the gallery.

I heard his metal box slam shut.

Karin watched me put Ned's card back into my wallet.

"You have a lot of nerve," she said. "How'd you get that, borrow it from a friend or bonk somebody on the head for it? If I'd known you were getting in for the student rate, I'd have let you pay for me."

We began eyeing the paintings, standing side by side, then straying apart, then reconverging. At first I simply examined each picture for any imperfection I could find. Then I realized it was more interesting to put my face about an inch away from each picture. This not only allowed me to see the individual brush strokes of the artist, but it made the guy at the front desk very nervous, because evidently part of his job was making sure you didn't put your grubby fingers all over the pictures. I found that if I raised my hand and reached out a few inches from the painting, he cleared his throat. I wondered what would happen if I actually touched a picture. He'd probably start retching.

Every chance I got, I looked at Karin. I caught a glimpse of her ears. Her earrings were miniature Space Needles.

We spent over an hour there. When we came back outside, it was overcast and raining. It was almost four o'clock. We started walking toward the north end of campus, having agreed to go somewhere for a snack.

We walked slowly and didn't say much, which was fine with me. I was used to three sisters and a mother who thought a gap in conversation was more painful than a toothache. But Karin seemed more like me, content just to walk and look around and think her thoughts.

"Do you live alone?" I asked her.

"No."

"With your family?"

"I guess Betty's my family," she said.

"Betty?"

"She's my grandmother. Not my real grandmother, but as close as you can get."

"Do you have parents?"

"Parents, aunts, and uncles—every one of them mad."

"Mad crazy or mad angry?"

"Mad, furious. At me. We had what you might call a major rift. Unfixable and permanent."

We left the campus and found a coffee shop. As I started to pull the door open for her, I stopped suddenly and she almost ran into it.

"Sorry," I said. "I just had a thought. Maybe you get enough of coffee shops."

She laughed and put her hand on my arm. "I'm fine as long as I don't have to wait on anybody." She added with a smile, "Or hear anybody ask me if that cat is all we have for dessert."

I called her the next day and she answered on the second ring.

"Hi," I said.

"Hi!"

"What are you doing?"

"Eating toast. How about you?"

"Standing here looking out the window," I said. "How was work last night?"

"Fine, except you didn't show up."

"You'd seen enough of me for one day."

"Not true," she said. "What do you see out your window?"

"Telephone wires," I said.

"Thank goodness for those," she said.

"Unless you're using a cordless phone," I said.

"What else do you see?"

"People. Bicycles. Mountains. Mud puddles. Rain. Is it raining in Wallingford?"

"Let's see—yep, it's raining in Wallingford."

"What's on your toast?" I asked.

"Jam."

"What kind?"

"Raspberry."

"What brand?"

"Betty's brand. It's homemade."

"Ah. She even makes jam. Wanna do something before you go to work?"

"Can't today," she said. "Betty needs me around here. How about tomorrow? It's my night off."

"Sounds good. Betty won't need you?"

"Nope. I'm free and clear."

"So am I," I said.

After I hung up, I stood looking out the window at the people below, the cars, buses, telephone wires. I repeated those three words aloud, and I liked the sound of them.

So am I.

Fifteen

FOR OUR THIRD DATE, Karin finally told me her Wallingford address, so I could drive over and pick her up.

She was waiting for me on her front porch, her knees together, feet on the first step, hands in the pockets of the same rain jacket she'd worn to the art gallery. When I pulled alongside the curb, she came down the walkway to my car and got in.

"Hey, you shaved," she said. "Let's check it out." She leaned over and kissed my cheek. It was the first time she'd done so, and for some reason it made me blush. "Very nice," she said. "Smooth as a baby's whatever."

"So, uh, that's where you live, eh?" I said, looking past her to the two-story house.

"That's it."

"Well-kept place," I said.

I let the brake off and put the car into gear, but Karin touched my arm and said, "Hold it a second."

I shifted back into neutral. She was biting her upper lip.

"What's up?" I asked.

She didn't answer. We sat idling for a minute. She turned and faced me, and I had the feeling that she was trying to look inside me. I wondered if I was about to hear some bad news. She stopped chewing her upper lip, leaned back in the seat, and sighed deeply. "I've been rude," she said.

"You have?"

"Yes. I haven't even asked you to come in and be introduced."

Two minutes later I was meeting Betty and a one-year-old named Devin, who clung to Betty's polyester pants leg and stared at me.

"He's never seen anyone quite so tall," Betty said genially. "His father is rather on the short side."

Devin peeked at me from behind Betty's leg. I bent toward him with my hands on my knees. "Hello, boy." He burrowed his face into Betty's leg.

While Betty and I made polite chitchat, I surveyed the living room. It had the unmistakable look and smell of a grandma's house, yet at the same time it was strewn wall-to-wall with cars, trucks, balls, puzzles, picture books, and stuffed animals.

On the coffee table facing the TV was a large soft-cover book that read G.E.D./High School Equivalency Preparation and Practice Tests. There was a pencil in the book. Beside the book was a piece of notebook paper that had been numbered 1 to 40, and about half the numbers had a letter next to them.

On top of the TV was a photograph that I could see clearly from where I stood. It was Karin sitting on a couch next to a long-haired heavy-metal dude who looked about sixteen. They both wore ragged jeans and had their feet up on the coffee table. The guy was grinning, his arm around Karin, and she had her chin raised slightly in a laughing way. His hair practically covered the entire upper half of his face. His teeth were crooked.

Karin saw what I was looking at.

"That's Richie," she said.

"You look happy," I said.

Soon we were driving down the street in my Volvo.

"Devin sure has your eyes," I said.

"I almost kept him a secret from you."

"Why would you do that?"

"Can't you guess?"

"No, not really."

She smiled and rested her hand on my shoulder. "Come now. Don't you feel strange going out with a mother?"

"As long as she's not *my* mother."

She was looking at me with narrowed eyes and a slight smile.

"What?" I said.

"Oh, I can't figure out whether you're *very* simple-minded or just a little."

"Let me know when you do," I said. "So, this Richie's the father?"

Karin nodded. "He's Betty's grandson. My ex-boyfriend."

"You live with your ex-boyfriend's grandmother?"

"Yeah, but Betty's more than that. I mean, she's Devin's great-grandmother. And she's—I don't know what I'd do without Betty. She does everything."

"Where's Richie?"

"He comes and goes."

"Does he live there?"

"He visits when he's in town. He lives on the road."

"On the— You mean on the street?"

She laughed. "On the road. Motels. He's in a band. He's the bass player."

"What's their name?"

"Flex."

"You're kidding."

"You've heard of them?"

"They played at my graduation dance. Hey, they're pretty good."

She sighed. "Well, they're still waiting for their big break."

"Everybody's waiting for something. You said that."

"They do keep busy, though," Karin said. "Dances, county fairs, bars, that sort of thing."

"So Richie doesn't have much time to be a daddy?"

"Not much time and not much interest. And no training—he never had one of his own."

"A dad? Oh."

We drove on.

"Well," I said, "I guess I know the long version now."

"Pretty much."

"My mental math isn't so good. Were you pregnant when you quit school?"

"Three months."

"But that wasn't why you quit?"

"No. I already told you why I quit."

"Well, look," I said, "you shared something about yourself with me, and I'm glad you did."

"Are you?"

"Yes. And now I think I should share something with you."

"Some big dark secret?" she asked, smiling.

"Well, dark, but not all that big."

"You mean compared to mine?" she said.

"No, yours is living. Mine's more of a . . ."

"Skeleton in the closet?"

"More like a corpse. You might be just the person to help me bury it."

"Tell me about it," she said.

"I'll show you."

We drove north, through Nimbus Creek, up the winding road to my old baseball glory field. We parked, got out, and walked past the spot where Dick Drago and I had sat two months ago eating tangerines. It was too wet to sit there now. Besides, we both preferred walking in the gentle rain.

While we walked I spun the saga of Dean Duffy's rise and fall. The beginning. Jack Trant. Little League. The purple "R" card. The incredible, monumental 507-foot home run off of J. L. Bean. The good old Gravediggers. Lompoc, the Cubans, the four girls. The sore arm. The two-year slump. The summer on San Juan Island.

That's where I stopped. I didn't tell her about Drago and his offer. At that moment I almost wished the offer had never been made. I didn't want to think about going anywhere. I wanted everything to stay just as it was.

And for the next two weeks everything really did seem to pause. Karin and I saw each other every day. It wasn't any passionate whirlwind romance; in a way, I was glad of that, and even proud of it, because I'd never known a girl, other than maybe Rose, that I so much enjoyed just being with and touching and talking to without any pressure. I simply felt good being with Karin, the way I felt when I heard a song I liked, or when I was in the middle of a good round of golf. Not like playing baseball, though. In baseball, I always had to be pushing myself, both mentally and physically, beyond the comfort level. To have just relaxed and enjoyed the moment while I was hitting or pitching or playing first base would have gotten me benched in a hurry.

So for a while Karin and I just coasted, but I knew it was only temporary. We spent much of the time telling our "story," our history, and when Karin talked about Richie, about the things they had done together or the things they both liked, a certain light came into her eyes, and I knew that some part of her was waiting for him.

I was waiting for something, too, although I wasn't sure what it was. So, in a way, that's what Karin and I did together: we waited for whatever was meant to happen in our lives to happen.

Sixteen

"WHERE'VE YOU BEEN keeping yourself, stranger?" Jack asked.

It was Friday night, December 3. Jack and Shilo and I were playing pool in the billiard room, straight pool, a penny a ball. Shilo, of course, was killing us.

"Well," I said, busying myself a little more than necessary with racking the balls for Shilo's break, "believe it or not, I've been seeing a girl."

"She must be something," Jack said, watching Shilo knock in two balls on her break. "You not only turned down my last golf invitation, you've even been shaving."

"Well, I think it's great news," Shilo said. "You look better than you have for weeks, Dean."

"Just don't let her go complicating your life," Jack said. "Women have a way of distracting us men. They have a way of making us take our eyes off the mark."

Shilo gave him a sharp glance, then continued circling the table, choosing her shots. She sank three, four, five in a row.

"Once you get mixed up with women," Jack said, "you might as well kiss your—"

Shilo slammed the 15 ball into the side pocket with amazing force. "Kiss your what, dear?" she said.

"Ambitions," he said. "Kiss your ambitions goodbye."

"Thank you very much," Shilo said.

"I was referring to my first wife," Jack said, "not you. But, speaking of ambitions, Drago called me the other night. We had a long talk, mostly about you, Dean. It's getting down to the wire, you know, son."

"I know," I said.

"No need to panic yet, but the sooner Drago has an answer, the better. He'll be giving you a call pretty soon."

Jack cleared his throat and frowned. I think he was fighting the urge to ask me if I'd made a decision.

Shilo must have seen it, too, because she broke in with "By the way, Dean, we got a postcard from Ned and Rose."

"Oh, yeah, so did I," I said.

It had come a few days ago from London. The Changing of the Guard. I wondered if Ned had intended some symbolism in that. He'd written: "Less than a month to go! Can't wait! How are all my little munchkins?"

His little munchkins were doing all right. A few of the fish seemed dead, but you never could be sure with fish.

Three days later—Monday, December 6—Dick Drago telephoned me at the apartment.

"I need to know," he said. "I need an answer. I've got

business in Seattle this Sunday. I'll just be passing through. Jack and Shilo said we can meet at their house. I'll have the letter of intent with me and you'll have to make your decision then. One o'clock at the Trants' this Sunday. That okay?"

"That's fine," I said. "See you Sunday."

The week went slowly. I began having dreams that I hadn't had since the depths of my batting slump. Baseballs thrown at my head. Bats too heavy to swing or too slippery to hold. A pitch comes at me, I swing and connect, but when I try to run to first, my legs are in quicksand. In these dreams, Dick Drago's giant face looms behind pitcher's mound like Mt. Rainier. Sometimes it's the smirking face of J. L. Bean instead of Drago's.

On Friday, a little before noon, I was walking across the UW campus, intending to have a Huskyburger at the Hub cafeteria, when I spotted that baseball player from Western Thought class. The purposeful way he walked led me to believe that he had only one thing on his mind: lunch.

I followed him. He went north through the campus, jaywalked across 45th Street, and continued along Greek Row, where the fraternity and sorority houses were.

Why was I following him? Why did I feel the need to find out more about him? I was only forty-nine hours away from having to make the most important decision of my life, and something was telling me that this guy might be able to help.

Next thing I knew, I was hurrying alongside him.

"You played baseball in high school, didn't you?" I asked.

He kept walking but slowed down, eyeing me. He was chewing a big wad of bubble gum. "Yap," he said.

"Was it Evergreen? Did you play third base for Evergreen?"

"I played third," he said, "but not for Evergreen. I'm from Boise, Ida—"

Suddenly his expression changed. His face lit up.

"Dean Duffy! Hey!" He grabbed my hand and shook it vigorously. "Hey! I don't believe it. You know who I am? No, I wouldn't expect you'd remember me! You struck me out three times in one game. Three times! I'm Woods. Pete Woods."

"Pete Woods . . ." I said, thinking.

"You pitched for Sarah Chipman," Woods said. "The year you guys went all the way at Lompoc. I played for the Boise Brios."

"I remember the Brios," I said. "We played you in the Regionals. In Eugene, Oregon."

"That's right!" He nodded energetically.

"The Brios," I repeated. "Nobody on our team knew what a brio was. Not even our coach. We kept saying, 'What's a brio?' It turned into a big joke. To this day, you can go up to any Gravedigger and make him crack up just by saying 'What's a brio?' in a certain voice."

Woods laughed hard. This gave me time to study his face and try to recall him and the rest of his team. "I remember your pitcher," I said. "Clancy Albers, wasn't it?"

"That's right," Woods said. "Poor Clance! You guys shelled him that day. The Gravediggers were awesome. You beat us seven-zip. God, I remember you at the plate, man. You tore the cover off that ball. I remember all five of your at-bats. I mean, seriously, I *studied* your swing. You had one sweet swing. I'm a lefty like you."

"Pete Woods . . ." I was frustrated and embarrassed that I couldn't remember him. How could I forget a guy I'd struck out three times in one game? "You, uh, batted second in the lineup?"

"No, eighth," he said.

"Eighth? Oh."

No wonder I couldn't remember him. The guy must've had the kind of bat a pitcher didn't worry too much about.

"Do you still play baseball?" Woods asked.

I hesitated only a second. "No. You?"

"Sure do."

He told me everything as we walked along the sidewalk. He was a freshman, here on a baseball scholarship. A full four-year scholarship.

I couldn't believe it. A full ride. It stung me. I was envious as hell.

"No offense," I said, "but you must've really improved after that year with the Brios."

"Hey, you better believe it," he said.

"What was your secret?" I asked.

"Secret? Aw, I don't know. Studying guys like you, I guess. Busting my fanny, mostly. I sure didn't have no natural swing."

And here he is and here I ain't, I said to myself. What did he have that I didn't have?

Suddenly I knew I wanted to *be* this guy, to be doing exactly what he was doing. What a life he must have. Playing ball at a big university, everything paid for, all doors open to him. He belonged; he was in. Sure, he had the pressure to deal with, the possibility of failure, but he was doing it, he had made the decision and taken the leap. *That's* what he had that I didn't have.

Woods came to a stop at a walkway that led to the ornate front door of a frat house. He asked if I belonged to a fraternity. I told him no. He asked if I was thinking of joining one. I told him yes, and I meant it. I *did* want to belong to something.

He invited me in for lunch. The Pi Phi Somethings. We lined up in the kitchen and helped ourselves from a big kettle of beef stew. There were two long rectangular wooden tables, about twenty men per table. Woods and I sat down at one of them.

No one was allowed to eat yet. First, announcements. Woods stood up and said he had a "rushee," and the Pi Phis looked at me and pounded the table several times with their fists, which made the silverware jump.

Then a song had to be sung. One of the freshmen was called on and told to "keep it clean, we have a rushee." He cleared his throat and began croaking a song, which everyone joined in on. It was sung to the tune of "O Christmas Tree":

> *Tau Upsilon on bended knee*
> *Will kiss the ass of Sigma E,*
> *And Sigma E will turn about*
> *And kiss the ass of Alpha Delt;*
> *And Alpha Delt, before they die,*
> *Will kiss the ass of Old Pi Phi*
> *But Pi Phi ne'er will bend a knee*
> *To any damn fraternity.*

On the last note of the song they pounded the table, which made the silverware jump again.

Then we ate our beef stew.

After lunch, Woods showed me around the house. Several Pi Phis came up to shake my hand and invite me to the big "function" tomorrow night, which was what they called a party.

Woods walked me to the front door. We shook hands.

"By the way," I said, "you have Dr. Dona's class, don't you? 'Decline of Western Thought'? I don't have it, but I've sat in on it a few times and I think I saw you there. Do you like it?"

"Like what?"

"The class."

Woods shrugged. "It's okay."

"Do you take notes?" I asked.

"Notes? Yeah. Why?"

"I don't know. I guess I thought I might have seen you asleep in there."

He peered at me with a suspicious look. Then he just shrugged. "So?"

I shrugged. "I guess I was just wondering how you took notes."

"Doesn't matter," he said. "All I need is a C to keep my scholarship. I can pull down a C, no problem. Piece a cake." He looked left and right, then leaned toward me and lowered his voice. "The prof recycles the same old exams every year. One of the guys in the house took the class last fall. Kept all the exams."

I nodded. "Of course, you might learn something if you stayed awake."

"Don't get righteous on me, man," he said.

He had a point. Would I have been any different in his place? Hadn't I been that way through junior high and high school? Cruising through my classes, just getting by, hardly a clue as to what was happening in the world. I had believed you had to be that way if you wanted to be truly great, you had to devote your whole being to baseball and sacrifice everything else. The thought of that made me a little sick.

"What do I care about all this 'Decline of Western Thought' crap?" Woods said. "Who cares? You know that midterm we had last week? It was *identical* to the one Bean had last fall. He gave me his old copy and sure enough, same questions, word for word. I can breeze."

"Who did you say?"

"Huh?"

"Did you say Bean?"

"Yeah. He had the class last fall. Lucky for me he kept all the old exams."

"Jonathan Livingston Bean?"

Woods smiled. "You know Jelly?"

"Jelly?" I said.

"J. L. Bean. Jelly Bean. Everybody calls him that."

"He's in this house? I didn't see him at lunch."

"I think he eats first lunch," Woods said. "How do you know Jelly?"

"I played against him."

Woods stared. "Played?"

"Baseball," I said.

"No way," he said.

"Wait a minute," I said. "You mean you don't know?

He pitched for Stanton High School. J. L. Bean was only one of the best pitchers in the state."

Woods let out a laugh. "Get *outa* here! Now I've heard everything!"

"It's true," I said.

Woods was still shaking his head in disbelief. "Jelly? No *way*."

"Will he be at this function of yours tomorrow night?" I asked.

"He'll probably be around somewhere. Will he remember you? How about I tell him you're coming?"

"Tell him I'm coming," I said.

Seventeen

SATURDAY WAS DRIZZLY and foggy but mild for mid-December. Karin and I were walking along the sidewalk a few blocks from her house, past the big old Wallingford houses. She had called me earlier and asked me to come over, because she had something she wanted to talk to me about. I had a feeling I knew what it was.

"Richie's in town," she said.

I nodded. "How do you feel about seeing him?"

"Like my heart's up here." She touched her throat.

"How long is he in town?"

"Only till Tuesday. Then they drive up to Sedro-Wooley. They're playing between bouts at the Tag-Team Wrestling Marathon."

"Anything I can do?" I asked. "Stay out of the picture?"

"What? No. No, I want you to meet him."

"Richie?"

"He's kind of shy, but you'll like him."

"Meet him, eh?" I said, pondering it. "I'd like to meet Richie. When?"

"How about tomorrow?" Karin said. "They're playing at a roller rink in Bellevue." She smiled and looked at me. "Do you roller skate?"

"If it's deserted."

"It'll be packed," she said. "But we can go out afterward, the three of us."

"I'd like that," I said. "But tomorrow—I'm not sure about tomorrow." I felt a knot tighten in my stomach. "I have to meet somebody at one o'clock. Somebody I haven't told you about."

"A girl?"

"No. A man named Dick Drago. He's the head baseball coach at Shute College. He's offered me a one-semester baseball scholarship."

Karin stopped walking and faced me. "Seriously? That's great, isn't it?"

"It's only for one semester," I said.

"So what? When did you find out?"

"I've known the whole time I've known you."

She stared. "And you never said anything?"

"Well, I'll tell you, Karin. I'm kind of thinking I'll turn him down."

"Why?"

"Two reasons. For one thing, I've told you about my slump. I have no reason to believe I'll even be able to hit a baseball out of the infield."

"So you'll find out," she said.

"This is against college pitching, mind you," I added. "It's like graduating to level 2 when you've flunked level 1. Throw in a full load of tough college courses. And being away from home, in a strange place like eastern Washington. Why should I put myself through all that?"

"So it's fear, then," she said.

"What's fear?"

"Your reason for turning down the offer. I mean, I'm not blaming you, I'm just trying to understand. You're afraid you'll fail?"

"Karin, listen. You don't know what long walks are till you've walked back to the dugout after you've just struck out for the umpteenth time. I'm not even sure I could make the team. Getting cut is one of the few humiliations I've managed to avoid so far in my life. When somebody gives you a college scholarship, even if it's only for a semester, the least you can do is make the team. If I screwed up, it wouldn't just make *me* look bad. It'd make Jack and Dick Drago look like idiots. And if you really want to know the truth, sometimes when I think about *not* playing baseball anymore, I feel like it's a huge load off my shoulders."

"Then that's the other reason," she said.

"Huh?"

"You said you had two reasons for turning him down. The first was fear. We'll call it fear of screwing up and looking like a fool. The second is . . . relief? Relief that you don't have to find out whether you'd have screwed up and looked like a fool. The relief of giving up. I know that one well. It's always a relief to quit. Or to not even try. I have lots of firsthand experience at that."

"I'm not quitting anything," I said. "I'm starting over.

The only thing I want to quit is rubbing salt into this wound when it's trying to heal."

She smiled. "Rubbing salt, huh? I think that's called being alive."

"No."

"Yes. Dean, if you don't feel pain you're just . . . drugged. No pressures, no fears, no obstacles. Just a nice pleasant sleep. Never having to test yourself. Or decide what you're worth."

It made me think of Pitts. Not so much the part about being drugged, but about deciding what we're worth.

Karin and I had done a full circle, and we were back on her block.

"You know," she said, "Richie can be real butt and he's sure got a lot of growing up to do. But I give him credit for one thing: he's not afraid of doing what he really loves. He's not the world's greatest musician, and he hardly makes enough to cover traveling expenses, but he's *doing* it. He's still dreaming and he's still believing in himself."

"How about you?" I asked. "You obviously love the guy. The question is, do you believe in him?"

"That's not exactly the question," she said. "When you care for somebody, you always believe in them. I think the question is whether or not you accept them. I haven't figured that out yet—whether I can accept Richie the way he is."

"You're not really waiting for him, then," I said. "I'd been thinking you were waiting for him to make up his mind whether to be a father or whatever."

She looked at me. "I thought I was, too."

"But either you accept him or you don't, right?" I said. "So you can't wait for him to be somebody else."

"No," she said. "You're right. I guess what I've been waiting for is myself to realize that I have to decide." She turned to me. Her eyes had become moist and very bright. "Boy, I had you all wrong. You're not simpleminded. Not one bit."

"Well, you were wrong about something else, too," I said. "About my reason for turning down that offer. It's you."

She looked away. "Uh-oh."

"No, wait—I don't mean—I'm not saying I've fallen madly in love with you or anything. I think I've known all along that you really care for Richie. I'm talking about the life I've had this fall. I've *liked* it. The apartment and the part-time job and being around the campus—I really think I could see myself being a student at the UW. And when you came along—you've been the best part of it. Starting with that very first night I walked into the Hasty Tasty and saw you behind the counter."

"I've liked being with you, too," she said. "Very much. But I think we've liked it because—well, because it's been so easy. It hasn't taken any effort or risk. You're so laid back; I like that about you, Dean, but I think you need to be on fire for *something*, you know? I think you have to do more than just hang out and cruise along, don't you think? One of my favorite things we've done was just going for drives without any destination. But you can't live your whole life that way— you'll never get anywhere."

"I suppose not," I said.

"You don't get excited about too many things," she said.

"I guess not," I said. "But I'll tell you, I don't think I

mind being on even ground. I don't want to live on a roller coaster. Isn't that the way it is with you and Richie? I mean, you two are either way high or way low. Sure, the highs are great. In baseball I had some big highs. But the lows . . . they kill you."

"Yeah," she said, smiling, "but the highs make it all worth it, don't you think?"

"I don't know," I said. I thought for a second, remembering what Pitts and I had talked about in the parking lot after our golf game. "I guess they give you something to base your hope on," I said.

"Yes."

Standing on the sidewalk in front of her house, Karin and I were getting cold. She asked me to come inside, but I said I had to be going. I remembered that Jack and Shilo had invited me to their house for a salmon dinner before I went to the fraternity party.

"Hey, listen," I said, "I hope it works out for you guys."

She smiled. "That goes for you, too." She kissed my cheek and turned away from me, and I watched her go up the stairs to her front door.

Eighteen

JACK AND SHILO were both in good spirits during dinner. Especially Shilo. Something was up. Her
cheeks had a high rosy glow. I had heard somewhere
that sometimes women in good spirits with a high rosy
glow were pregnant. This thought hit me between the
eyes. It was incredible, but not impossible.

"Jack, I can't hold it any longer," she said. "I *have* to
tell him. Dean, we have some news."

Gently I lay down my fork. She couldn't be. No way.

Jack, who had finished eating, took on one of his gruff
scowls. "I'm in the mood for a scotch. Excuse me a
minute while I go find the Johnnie Walker."

He got up abruptly from the kitchen table and headed
for the liquor cabinet in the billiard room.

Shilo looked at me, still smiling. "He's embarrassed."

"Embarrassed?" I gave the back of my head a vigorous scratch.

"You know how he gets when he does something nice. He gets all embarrassed."

I stared, and could still only be an echo. "Something nice?"

Shilo nodded. "He's been in a weird mood all day. Kind of thoughtful and . . . brooding. He took a long walk by himself, then he just sat brooding in his study and didn't want any company and didn't even care about watching the golf on TV. A few minutes later, I heard him talking on the phone. Dean, do you know what he did?"

"What?"

"He called Van."

"He—" I looked away. The news wasn't anything to throw a person into shock, but I was startled. I stared off to the side of Shilo.

"He called Van in Santa Cruz," she said proudly. "Just called him right up out of the blue." She laughed breathily, shaking her head as if she still didn't quite believe it.

"No kidding," I said slowly.

"And, Dean, they *talked*. There wasn't any yelling or growling or fists slamming the table. Just a civilized conversation, *remotely* resembling a father-and-son exchange. And *here's* the incredible part. This is going to knock your socks off. We're flying down there in the morning. Tomorrow. We're flying to San Francisco and renting a car and driving to Santa Cruz. Van's going to be performing in a play tomorrow night. I forget the name of it, but he invited us to come and watch it. And

Jack said we'd do it. Just like that!" She laughed. "Can you even believe it? I don't know which is more shocking, Jack's calling him or Van's inviting us—or our dropping everything and *going*."

Jack returned, carrying a glass with ice and scotch in it.

"I just hope I don't sleep through the damn play," Jack said.

"You won't," Shilo said.

"It better not be a musical or one of those things where they strip down but you still can't tell what sex they are."

"Oh, don't worry," Shilo said. "Do you know how proud I am of him?" She rose from her chair and gave Jack a kiss on the cheek. "But now I have two million things to do before tomorrow morning. We're leaving at six! How about if you two clean up the kitchen while I finish packing."

Jack and I stayed seated at the kitchen table after she'd gone. He looked at his drink, swirling it around.

He glanced at his watch. "What time you planning to see Bean?"

"Whenever."

"Fraternity parties . . . Those were good times for me. I have a lot of fond—oh, never mind that. I called Drago and told him we'd be gone but that he's still welcome to come here. I told him where the key's hidden. It's just as well I won't be around when you two have your meeting. It's between you and him. I'm out of it."

Jack didn't sound entirely convinced. He leaned forward. "Dean, I made a promise to myself I'm not going to ask you what you've decided. I've been making imaginary speeches to you all fall. Giving all kinds of advice and lectures. All of it up here, in my own mind. Of course, I can't help but speculate a little on what you'll do. And in my business, whenever it takes a person forever to decide yes or no, it always ends up being no." He let out a long breath and didn't meet my eye, and I was glad of that. "But let's not talk about that. I'll just have to not worry about it, down there in Santa Cruz."

"What made you call Van?" I asked.

Jack shook his head and gave a short laugh. "All those imaginary lectures I've been giving you. All that advice. I guess I've really been giving it to *myself*. I've never spent much time listening to my own advice and lectures. But one thing I've always said is that the biggest difference between someone who's a success in life and someone who's a failure is how soon he gives up. Well, I'll tell you. I was always pretty quick to give up on Van. It was damn hard for me to be interested in the things he was interested in. But that was no excuse, even though I used it as one. It was real convenient just to throw up my hands and say, 'Well, if *he's* not going to try, then why should I.' But I was his father. It was my damn job to try harder and keep on trying. And I think Van *did* try, Dean, I think he did, and I didn't give him much of a chance."

"I didn't help things," I said. "I took up your time. I knew what I was doing. Competing with Van."

Jack shook his head. "No. I was using you. It's that old cliché, I hate to admit it: the tired old ex-jock . . . I've spent the last ten years trying to grab some glory through you, Dean. I groomed you to be a baseball player because I figured it was too late to groom myself to be anything new. Well, maybe it is and maybe it isn't."

I swallowed, my throat swelling. "You and Shilo have given me a lot. I don't want to disappoint you again."

"Dean, I'm trying to tell you that I called Dick Drago more for myself than for you. You don't owe me or Shilo a thing. And you *didn't* disappoint me, son. Never. Hell, I was *proud* of you. You were in there swinging to the very end. Do I need to remind you that I was one of those three remaining spectators that last game of the season? You struck out on the last pitch of the *season*. And you took one hell of a cut at it. You went down fighting."

I smiled. "I did, didn't I. I thought I had it nailed, too."

"So did I," Jack said. "Now how about let's get this kitchen cleaned up."

Nineteen

WHEN I GOT TO THE FRATERNITY, I spent the first fifteen minutes wandering around. I saw neither Pete Woods nor anyone who looked like Bean. There were people everywhere, but it sounded like the real partying was going on in the basement.

I got nabbed in the living room by the house president, whose name was Lomas. He had a mustache and a suit and tie; the tie was loosened. He looked like a stud.

"Duffy," he said, "if you have time later, I'd like to talk to you about joining our house."

"Sure," I said. "Except I'm not a student yet."

He looked puzzled. "Not a— But I thought yesterday Woods said—" He shrugged. "Oh well. That's what I get for expecting Woods to get something straight."

"It's not Woods's fault," I said. "I sort of misled everybody yesterday."

"Well, are you considering being a student at the UW?" Lomas asked.

"Definitely," I said. "I've got it narrowed down to two choices, the UW and Shute College."

Lomas looked impressed. "Shute, huh? Excellent school. Have you been accepted there?"

I nodded. "They've offered me a baseball scholarship for one semester. I'm seeing the coach tomorrow at one o'clock. I have to decide whether or not to sign the letter of intent. I haven't even decided yet. I don't know what I'm going to do . . ."

Lomas nodded and glanced at his watch. I realized that I was telling this to a complete stranger. Was that how desperate I'd gotten? If he'd given me another two minutes, I probably would have had him making the decision for me.

"Well, that's great, Duffy, that's great. Just remember our door is always open. Please excuse me . . . Oh, Duffy, by the way," he said, "Jelly knows you're coming. Woods told him last night at dinner. Just go up to the third floor and head down the hall. Ask anybody you see, they'll point you, everybody knows where Jelly is. Have fun, Duffy. Good luck."

I found Bean in a low-ceilinged room that reeked of tea. He and three other people—two guys and a girl— were playing cards.

I barely recognized him. The nickname Jelly was apt. He wasn't exactly fat, but jellified from head to toe. His face was bloated, his hair long and stringy and combed straight back, with a lock of it falling forward. His wire-rimmed glasses were the same type he'd worn four years ago.

When he saw me, he seemed to recognize me instantly. He laid his cards face-down on the table. "Big D," he said. "D squared. Come in. Good to see you. Can you guess what we're playing?"

"Poker?"

It was a dumb guess; there weren't even any chips on the table. Understandably, all four players snickered.

Bean stood up from the table. "Count 'em up, folks. We'll have a recess and reconvene in one hour. My old nemesis and I have some talking to do."

Bean's face had only a vestige of that arrogance and cockiness that had intimidated and enraged so many batters. Despite his chubbiness, he seemed smaller than he used to, somewhat deflated.

"Follow me," he said. "I've got the perfect place for us to have a quiet chat. If you don't mind freezing your fanny off."

Bean led the way up a narrow, almost vertical set of stairs—more like a ladder than stairs. At the top was a ceiling door at a forty-five-degree angle. Bean gave it a push and we climbed through it, out onto the roof, a kind of sun deck. It wasn't raining but misty, and the wooden planks we stood on were slick and mildewed.

"Can't see much in this fog," Bean said, "but on a clear day it's one of the finest views in town. We encourage the ladies to sun themselves up here. It's very private and they often remove their bikini tops. On a hot spring day you'll find a row of topless beauties sunbathing."

"Is that what you meant by one of the finest views in town?" I asked.

He chuckled artificially. Then he took out a pipe and went through the elaborate process of tamping it with Prince Albert tobacco. I watched him for about five minutes, until he finally fired it up.

"You're not really a rushee," he said, drawing the pipe. "You're not even a student here."

"That's true," I said. "How'd you know?"

"Back in August, some half-baked pothead who knew you told me you had moved to the San Juan Islands. Which would make for a rather long daily commute to the UW. Why aren't you downstairs in Little Hell, getting drunk with the other pretend-rushees?"

"I'm not pretending anything," I said.

"You did to Woods. Why? Were you that hard up for a free lunch?"

"Woods is a baseball player," I said. "Baseball players interest me. Especially Woods."

"Kindred spirits," Bean said sarcastically. "How quaint."

"Yeah," I said. "I do a lot of quaint things. Don't you?"

Bean ignored this. "Why did you come here tonight, Duffy?"

"To see you."

"I'm honored."

"You look it."

"Why did you want to see me?" he asked.

"I'm looking for something, I guess. Some answers."
Bean groaned. "Oh, Lord."

"Actually," I said, "that half-baked pothead Pitts told

me you were asking about me and had something to say to me. By the way, I don't think he's a pothead anymore."

"How lovely," Bean said. "I'm sure they're all cheering in his rehab program."

"Man," I said, shaking my head and smiling, "you haven't changed."

This brought the old smirk to Bean's face. "Oh, but I *have*, Duffy. I'm only a shadow of the arrogant bastard I was three and a half years ago. How about you? Have you changed over the years?"

"I think so."

"For better or worse?"

"That I don't know," I said.

"I suppose the question is irrelevant," Bean said. "Is it too cold up here for you?"

"Not at all." I was freezing.

"Good. So here we are, Bean and Duffy, high atop the Pi Phi house. Two has-been baseball players. Four years ago, it was a different story. It was the whole *world* we were on top of. At least I was; you were only a ninth-grader, shooting to the top. We couldn't lose. Didn't it seem that way to you, Duffy?"

I nodded. "I guess."

"And now look at us. Big-time losers. Ain't no fun anymore, is it? I've kept very close track of you over the years, Duffy. I've followed your career with the greatest of interest. I was getting ready to start my sophomore year in college when I watched you throw a two-hitter against Cuba on nationwide TV. My God, I hated you that day. You were on the fast track to the Major Leagues. But something happened to you after that

World Championship game. You came unraveled, just as I had a year and a half before that. Would you like to know what ruined me, Duffy?"

"Sure."

"You did, Duffy."

"What do you mean, I did? How did I ruin you? You can't mean the home run I hit off you?"

"The grand slam, yes. Oh, yes, the grand slam."

"You're crazy," I said. "You're trying to tell me you gave up one grand slam and it ruined your life? Come on, Bean."

"Calm down, Duffy. I'll explain. It's what I've wanted to tell you for quite a while now. I know it sounds absurd. But, you see, it's all a matter of what a person believes. Every pitcher gives up at least one grand slam, right? Of course. It certainly shouldn't represent a major catastrophe in that pitcher's life. He shrugs it off and keeps going. But I wasn't able to do that."

"And that's my fault?" I said.

"Of course not, but I've just told you, it's all a matter of what a person believes. I believed it *was* your fault."

Bean paused, filled his lungs with night air. Below, in the alley, I heard shouts, a scuffle, a beer bottle breaking, somebody getting slammed against a Dumpster, somebody grunting as if being slugged. I went to the railing and looked down, but I couldn't see that section of the alley. I turned and looked at Bean. He stood puffing his pipe, staring at nothing, as if he hadn't even heard the commotion.

"Look, Duffy," he said. "You have to realize something. Long before you hit that home run, my life was teetering on the edge of a morass. All it needed was one push to send it over the edge. You gave the push. I held *you* responsible, I blamed *you*. I fully admit that wasn't rational, but—listen, I'm not making much sense. Bear with me, please. Let me see if I can explain a little more coherently."

Bean held his pipe to his mouth and began. "I know what I was back then," he said. "An extremely obnoxious, cocky, arrogant bastard. But it was all an act. Deep down, I was scared. I was terrified. Full of self-doubt. There were only two things that gave me confidence. One was booze. The other was a certain pitch I had invented myself. An absolutely unhittable pitch. My secret weapon."

"The Beanerball," I said, unable to keep from smiling.

"That's what other people called it, not what I called it. I called it . . . well, I didn't call it anything. It was my security blanket. I pulled it out only when I really needed it. My catcher was the only other person who actually knew about the pitch. There was a lot of talk and rumor and speculation, but nobody except my catcher and I knew. I would give my catcher a special signal when I was going to throw it. The pitch was illegal. It involved doctoring the ball. If I'd been caught, I would have been kicked off the team for good. I suppose my catcher would have, too. Fortunately, I had the same catcher all through high school, which was when I developed the pitch. By my senior year I had finally worked it out to perfection.

"Trouble is," Bean went on, "I started to rely on it more and more. The more I used it, the better I looked. The better I looked, the more people expected of me. That pitch was like a drug.

"But one day I threw the pitch to you and you sent it to kingdom come. Shrug it off? I thought the pitch was infallible. The pitch was my confidence, and now that was shaken. It seemed to me that people were looking at me . . . differently. Were they smirking at me? Not showing me as much respect? I was probably just imagining it, but you see, when you begin to doubt, your imagination starts working overtime. So I really *did* start to alienate people.

"I fulfilled my own prophecy. I relied more and more on the illegal pitch. Of course, the more I threw it, the greater my chances of getting caught. It's truly amazing that I *didn't* get caught, but I grew more paranoid. Which made me less effective as a pitcher, which made me have to rely even more on the 'Beanerball,' which made me more nervous and scared that it was just a matter of time until I got caught. Which made me drink more. The more I drank, the more horrible I acted toward my girlfriend and friends and teammates. It didn't take long to lose my friends, and my girlfriend dumped me. She dumped me for my catcher!

"But do you see, Duffy, do you see how the whole lousy thing was connected? All it took was one blow to trigger it. And that blow came from *you*. I absolutely hated your guts. I can look back on it now and see how irrational I was. I was just using you as an excuse.

"In spite of it all, I managed to graduate with decent grades and get accepted to the UW and become a member of this fraternity. I drank my way through three years of college. I've maintained a 2.7 grade point average, but I do not remember a single class.

"And all the time I was destroying myself, I was thinking of the person responsible for it: Dean Duffy. And I'd say, 'I owe it all to you, Duffy. You are the cause of all this.'

"After a series of ugly incidents, which I don't need to go into, I was forced to enter a treatment facility. That was back in July. I've been dry almost five months. And I've wanted to talk to you. I've *needed* to see you. Because for three years or so I hated you and was even thinking of revenge. I actually planned to come after you. But two things stopped me. One was that in spite of how much I wanted revenge, when it came right down to it I didn't have the guts. The other thing that stopped me was that you seemed to be doing a lovely job of destroying your own career, for whatever reason. I took great delight in watching you fall apart. Maybe I even believed I was willing it to happen.

"Lovely, isn't it? But as I say, it's all over now, and I need to put it to rest. It's the last thing I need to do before I really feel like I'm starting over. Of course I don't blame you anymore. I know that everything that happened I brought on myself. I suppose deep down I always knew that. Even before you hit that home run, I knew I was on the edge, and I knew something could come along and push me. I just used you as an excuse."

Bean finished, and he was staring down at the deck. He hardly looked at me during his speech, and it made it easier for me to study his face in the semi-darkness as he spoke. His pipe had gone out. He tapped it on one of the wooden deck chairs. He glanced at his watch and I couldn't see what time it was, but it seemed he'd been talking for a long time.

"I kind of envy you," I said.

He was surprised. "Why, in God's name?"

"Because at least you know why it happened. I don't have a clue. You know you only have yourself to blame. But what can I blame? What did I do to bring it on?"

Bean shook his head. "I don't blame myself, Duffy. I take responsibility for everything that's happened in my life, but I don't *blame* myself for it. There's a difference. If there's one thing I've learned from this whole ordeal, it's that you have to take responsibility for whatever happens in your life, regardless of whether it's your 'fault' or not. All kinds of crap may fall on you for no apparent reason, as a result of nothing that you've done. But you still have to take responsibility, because, after all, it's your life, and if you're not responsible, who is? You say, 'All right, it's happened, I may not like it, but I can't undo it, so let's figure out what the hell to do from this point.' God, Duffy, if I had done that the day I gave up the grand slam, I'd be . . ."

Bean shook his head without finishing.

"Can I ask you a question?" I said.

"Fire away."

"That pitch of yours. The Beanerball. What was it? How'd you throw it?"

He smiled. "Asking me to divulge a trade secret? That's like asking a magician to . . . Ah, well. No reason to keep it a secret anymore. I used a tack."

"A tack?"

"A tack. Nothing more. I stuck a white thumbtack into the baseball."

"A tack," I repeated.

"A white thumbtack."

I surprised myself by laughing. "You ruined perfectly good baseballs with a tack."

"And never got caught," Bean said. "High school

153

umps, at least the ones in our league, were incredibly naïve. I stuck the tack in at precisely the right spot and a little crookedly, so that it didn't lie flat. I could just get part of my finger around it. It produced a sort of slider-sinker-knuckler that came right at your face and then dropped into the strike zone. Oh, God, it was a beautiful pitch. Absolutely un-bloody-hittable. The hours I spent perfecting it! And what made it almost foolproof was that if the ump got suspicious and wanted to inspect the ball, either I or my catcher, whoever had the ball, could pull the tack out in a wink. No trace of anything except the tiny hole."

Bean shook his head sadly. "You really belted it that day, Duffy old boy. You bloody parked it. A lousy butt-head freshman ninth-grader! You hit it a mile. I'll be damned if it didn't almost clear that outer fence."

I hesitated. "It did clear the outer fence."

He laughed. "You know very well it didn't."

"I know very well it did," I said.

"You couldn't see it, Duffy, nobody could. It went past the light towers. It disappeared in the darkness."

"I saw it," I repeated.

This time Bean tittered a little uncomfortably, as if unsure of my sanity. "Yes, well, if you want to believe you saw the ball go over the fence, that's fine, don't let me stop you. Look, ah—" He glanced again at his watch. "Good Lord, I should get back."

He left shortly after that. I stayed where I was, looking out at the night. The fog had gotten denser and had a moisture that beaded up on my hair. The night was quiet and still. It was too early for the hard-core partiers to call it a night, but they, as well as the band, must have been taking a break. All was peaceful, and I was alone with the fog.

Of all the things Bean had said, the one that stuck in my mind was that I was a loser and a has-been. Could a loser have done the things I'd done? Could a loser have stepped up to the plate and hit a baseball 507 feet, over the second fence and into a ravine? Did it matter? No. Yes. I guessed it mattered. I guessed they all mattered, every ball I'd ever swung at.

Why had I accepted so easily that I was destined to stay a failure?

Maybe I was washed up, maybe I wasn't. That didn't seem to make any difference right now. So what mattered? What really mattered? Maybe it was simply this: to know what I was worth.

Twenty

I AWOKE AT EIGHT O'CLOCK the next morning to the sound of mild Seattle rainfall.

I spent the next hour tending the fish and the plants, reminding them that Ned and Rose would be home in only seven days—December 20. I will be gone for good, I told them. They seemed to perk up.

I sat down in the kitchen nook and drank an orange juice while trying to think about the day that lay before me.

But I couldn't concentrate. I kept seeing Bean's face as it had been the night before, and hearing his voice: *. . . a lovely job of destroying your own . . .*

. . . If you're not responsible, who is?

Last night, things had seemed clearer to me: it was time to take control of my life; I could be more than just someone who drove around and remembered his glory days.

But today things didn't seem quite so simple. The old fear was creeping in. I needed one more push.

There were four hours until I'd be meeting with Drago. The more I thought about it, the tighter the knot in my stomach got. The fear . . .

I stood up, went to the sink, and rinsed my glass. I sure wasn't going to sit around for four hours.

I remembered the Seahawks were playing back east in Philadelphia today. The kickoff would be in about an hour, ten o'clock Pacific time. I decided I'd put on my sweats and drive out to the rubble heap and do a load. I would listen to the game on the car and truck radios. Afterward, if I felt like it, I could do some running. Four, five, six miles, whatever. After that, take a shower at Jack and Shilo's and put on the spare sweats I always kept in my trunk. Then wait for Drago to show up.

It wasn't a great plan, but at least it was a plan.

On the road, with the rain splattering my windshield and my wipers flapping back and forth, I changed the plan. At first I just drove without any destination. But, as Karin had said, if I did that I wouldn't end up any-where. Gradually I knew where I was going: Nimbus Creek Field. Why I was going to the baseball field, or what I'd do when I got there, I had no idea.

Twenty minutes later, I pulled into the huge empty parking lot. The whole park was deserted; I had it all to myself.

I got out in the rain and did some stretching, intend-ing to go for a run on the jogging path. But instead I found myself walking up to the baseball field. I stood in front of the bleachers watching the raindrops fall on the infield, glazed with water that reflected the gloomy sky.

The air smelled of grass and forest and mud. There was not much wind. The only sound was the rain drumming on the aluminum bleachers and on the wooden rooftops of the dugouts.

I put my hands on the cold wet chain-link fence and pressed my forehead against it, the way Bean's moll used to do so that Bean could kiss her.

Then I walked around the first-base dugout onto the infield, toward home plate. My tennis shoes left footprints on the infield. Home plate and the batter's box were under water.

I concentrated very hard for a minute. It took a lot of effort. My head was already wet from the rain, but this did not distract me. Soon I could see Bean on the mound, and I remembered the feeling I'd had that he was going to throw me his Beanerball. I saw the ball come toward my face and drop into the strike zone. I felt the impact of the bat on the ball and saw the baseball flying out over right field. Squinting through the rain, I watched the trajectory of the ball. It went beyond the light towers at the foot of the hill, and disappeared over the outer fence.

But even though my mind's eye could see the ball clearing that outer fence, my eyes told me that it was impossible. The fence seemed a mile away.

I fixed my eyes on the spot where the baseball had gone over the fence, and marked it with an imaginary X. It was something I had learned from my caddying days.

I started jogging toward the X.

I reached the five-foot home-run wall and hopped over it between the advertisements for Elaine's Beauty School and Pete's All-American Garage. I trotted between the light towers and started up the grassy hill. At the top stood the chain-link. I found my imaginary X.

Every six feet along the fence was a yellow warning sign with black letters that said:

EXTREME DANGER. DO NOT GO BEYOND THIS POINT.

I stood at about where I had marked my X, peering through the fence, but now that I had come all the way up here, I felt ludicrous and wondered why I had done it.

Still, I spent a good fifteen minutes walking back and forth along the fence, scanning the ground on the other side.

And then I stopped.

I looked closer through the fence at an object about twenty feet away. I wasn't quite sure, but . . . I squinted. It was brown, spherical, wedged under a slab of granite boulder. It looked like . . .

I couldn't believe it. I grabbed the fence and shook it and stared hard. I was so excited I almost yelled.

Those were seams. I was looking at a baseball.

The one I had hit off Bean? Why not? It could have come off my bat and landed in that exact spot and sat there half buried for the past three and a half years. That wasn't a long time for a baseball to sit. Why shouldn't it sit there thirty years? Who'd notice it? Wedged under that rock, it wasn't visible from anywhere but where I happened to be standing. Who would stand here and look for a baseball? *I* had never done it

before, and I *hit* the thing. And even if someone happened to be walking along this fence and saw the ball,
who would climb a ten-foot fence with sixteen inches
of barbed wire at the top, then step out onto the edge
of a steep slope, all for the sake of fetching an old
baseball.

Of course, it might have been any old baseball. But
what if it was the one I hit?

My eyes traveled up the fence to the barbed wire. I
had seen people climb barbed-wire fences. It took long
legs, strong hands, balance. Not easy, but doable.

Getting over the fence and straddling the barbed wire
would be the hardest part, but you had to be careful
once you landed on the other side, because it was very
slippery and the ball was only about ten feet from the
edge of the ravine.

I looked up at the sky. Rain continued to fall fast.

For three and a half years, that relic had been sitting
there waiting for me to come along and find it. I could
give it to my kid, who'd hand it down to his kid. The
Duffy heirloom. A paperweight for posterity. Once
upon a time there was a baseball player named Dean
Duffy who . . .

Who would care?

Why did *I* care? Why did I need to know that I was
right, that I had hit Bean's pitch over the fence? No one
cared but me. But it did matter to me. Yes, it did.

I took one more look at the barbed wire, grabbed hold
of the fence, and started to climb.

Twenty-one

I JUMPED the last five feet and landed with a muddy splat.

The tips of my fingers were numb from clutching the fence. I had strained a groin muscle while straddling the barbed wire, but at least I had made it over without slicing my hands.

I was definitely going to find an easier way back.

I baby-stepped the next twenty feet down the gradual incline, trying to keep control of my footing by stepping on rocks and twigs instead of the slippery mud. The closer I got to the ball, the steeper and barer the slope.

It was still raining and there was thunder and lightning. For a few minutes the rain drove so hard and heavy it almost seemed the whole slope would wash away before I got to the baseball. I felt no disgrace in crawling the last five feet on my hands and knees.

I finally made it to the ball. Still on my knees, I gripped it and tried to pull it free, but it was stuck solid, and my fingers were so numb they couldn't get a tight enough grip on the baseball.

I pulled and pulled. The tips of my fingers still had no feeling. I dug around the ball to get a better grip, and finally I worked it loose.

I held it up in the pouring rain to examine it.

It was a perfectly round rock. God had fashioned that rock into a baseball as lovingly as Shilo sculpted her hamburger patties. Even the cracks resembled hand-stitched seams. It was beautiful work. A good joke. I should have been laughing my head off.

I was suddenly furious. Not at the rock, but at myself. I was in a red rage. I was the maddest I'd ever been in my life, and I knew precisely why.

I scrambled to my feet and roared, reared back, and threw the baseball-rock as far as I could out into the ravine. Being a left-hander, I followed through with my weight on my right foot, which came down on a rock. My ankle turned and my foot skidded out from under me. I lurched forward. For a few seconds I fought for my balance, both running in place and doing a kind of marionette dance. But I lost the fight, flopped onto my back, and skidded the next ten feet over the edge of the slope.

I slid on my back another twenty or so yards down the slippery bank, grabbing at any rock or twig I passed and digging my hands and feet into the muddy slope. This slowed me enough so that I could catch hold of a twig. The twig held; I stopped. Clutching that three-foot twig, I turned over on my stomach and burrowed my feet into the mud, which was actually a combination of mud and slippery clay. The twig and my footholds were the only things keeping me from sliding the remaining two hundred feet to the bottom of the ravine. I couldn't see to the bottom, but I was sure that somewhere beyond one of those dips I'd be greeted by boulders or trees.

I looked back up to the edge where I'd gone over. My body had left a slick trail, a channel. There was no way to climb back up the slope—it was too steep and slippery and there weren't enough hand- and footholds. It was the same problem to my left and right: just the steep hillside of mud and clay.

I turned my attention to where gravity wanted to take me: down. The rest of the slope was amazingly bare. My only choice was a controlled slide. If I kept my hands and heels dug in, I could probably keep from gathering too much speed. It would be no problem for about two hundred feet, but then you came to a dip and you couldn't see beyond. It might not be fun to slide two hundred feet only to be stopped by a tree or a boulder and shatter one or both of my legs. I could crawl for a while, but with no one around to hear my calls for help, I'd eventually die of exposure.

I panicked. For the first time in my life, death seemed a real possibility. It felt like a presence, waiting patiently and with complete detachment.

Taking deep breaths, I tried to calm down. The roots of the twig were straining but still held.

When the time came to start the slide, I wanted to be sitting up, so I flopped over and redug my heels into the mud.

I was more comfortable on my back, even though the rain needled my face. I had to keep my eyes closed, and closing my eyes helped me relax.

The rain made me kind of sleepy. Pleasant images came into my mind. I heard Shilo's voice congratulating me after I sank a birdie putt on the thirteenth hole. I saw her opening her arms to encircle me in a hug. I smelled her perfume and felt her warm breath on the back of my neck. Shilo . . . How strange and beautiful that name was to me just now.

Then I thought of Rose Whittick and her long silky hair.

I had heard or read that when you're dying of exposure you get sleepy and imagine you're in love with every woman who comes into your mind. By the time you get to your kindergarten teacher, it's all over.

I dug my heels in deeper and kept my eyes shut.

Once they found my car, it wouldn't take them long to find my body. There would be speculation as to why I had climbed the fence. Would they figure suicide? He killed himself because he was . . . Lonely? Afraid? Lovesick?

Maybe it was better to have them think it was suicide than for them to know the truth: he died fetching a rock that he mistook for a baseball. I chuckled.

Why had I felt so angry at myself when I found that rock? I remembered now. I knew why.

I had believed that baseball would tell me how much I was worth.

But just then it seemed clear that nothing could tell me how much I was worth. No object or achievement, no home run, no batting average or statistic. No person could tell me how much I was worth—not Jack or Shilo or Drago or Karin or my parents or anyone else. It didn't matter how many screwups or successes I had. Either you knew what you were worth or you didn't. If you knew, then you knew it was more than all the wins added together. And if you didn't know, then you had reason to be afraid.

I had been afraid. Ever since Dick Drago had made the offer and I'd faced the possibility of playing baseball again, I had been afraid. I had assumed I was afraid of the pain and humiliation of failure, of disgracing myself and embarrassing Drago and Jack; or afraid of the possibility that baseball didn't really mean all that much to me; or that it would mean *too* much to me and overshadow everything else in life. But it wasn't any of that. I knew it now. I understood with absolute clarity why I had been so afraid: I had not known how much I was worth.

And I thought: I'm worth no less than anybody—Pitts, Bean, Woods, Richie. I thought: It's my life, nobody else's. It's up to me. Karin was right, Pitts was right, Jack, Bean—even Ruta Waterfall! They'd all said it, one way or another: Don't just cruise along; life isn't worth anything unless you take your best shot, and keep taking it, no matter what happens. I didn't have to be the greatest baseball player in the world or make it my god; all I had to do was take the shot.

The twig was slowly uprooting from the ground. The fibers were snapping.

I sat up and let go of the twig and was sliding down the hill on my butt, feet-first, digging my heels, hands, and elbows into the mud, carving tracks. But still I was gathering speed, too much speed, and the wind and rain lashed my face.

Toward the bottom now, I saw a wall of boulders. I dug in with everything I had, trying to put on the brakes, but I was sliding too fast. I came to the last dip in the slope, and there was a sudden drop-off. I think I actually left the ground for a moment. My feet were straight out, but the first impact was a gigantic splash.

I seemed to be in one piece. Nothing twisted or broken.

I was in a ditch. It was about five feet wide, but I couldn't tell how deep, because it was full of mud and ooze and garbage, with a few inches of water on the surface. I could feel all kinds of objects under me—cans, bottles, tires, who knows what; they kept me from sinking but did not give me enough support so that I could get out. Something squiggled under me. I yelped and tried to move, but I was stuck in the ooze. With my hand I kept trying to grab something solid to push against, and my hand latched onto something round and hard. I lifted it out of the mud.

It was the rock I had thrown from above. I yelled and threw it as if it were a hot potato.

As I gathered my strength for another attempt to stand, my hand once again came to rest on something embedded in the mud. I pulled it out and swished it in the water to wash the mud and goo from it. Some chemical reaction had turned it a rust color, but I saw that it was a baseball. A round, rusted tack was stuck in it.

I laughed, closed my eyes, and fell back into the muck with a splash.

Twenty-two

IT TOOK ME A WHILE to work my way out of the mud to solid ground. Then I had to walk along the rocks a few hundred yards until I found a part of the slope that I could climb. It wasn't an easy climb; I had to go on all fours. My muddy clothes seemed to add an extra fifty pounds, and I had aches and bruises that I hadn't been aware of, along with that pulled groin muscle. The baseball was crammed into my back pocket.

I made it to the chain-link fence, but there was no way I was going to climb it again. I began walking along it, and after about a half mile I found a small hole under the fence that some industrious varmint had dug. It was mostly mud, so I was able to dig with my hands and increase the size of the hole. I slithered under the fence.

Eventually I made it back to my car. Thank goodness

I hadn't lost my keys, and had left my wallet locked in the trunk. I opened the trunk in search of my extra pair of sweats, searched everywhere, even inside my golf bag, but the sweats were nowhere. I must have worn them and forgotten to put them back in. I rummaged around the trunk for something to wrap myself in. I was in a hurry to get out of these putrid clothes. I found an old green sheet that I used to spread down on the cement when I had to crawl under the car to change the oil. It was greasy but dry. I peeled off every stitch of my clothes and wrapped the sheet toga-style around my sore body.

Even with the car heater on full blast, I was shivering and numb. I turned the radio on to find out what time it was. The Seahawks were having their post-game locker-room interviews. It must have been well after two o'clock. Drago would be long gone from the Trants' house, and I'd never see him again.

With my wipers going, I drove through the quiet residential streets to Jack and Shilo's house. I wanted to drive faster, but I figured, with my present appearance, this wasn't the best time to get nabbed by a Nimbus Creek cop.

Finally I reached the Trants' driveway. Unbelievably, a car was there, a red Buick Skylark, an Avis sticker on its rear bumper. As I pulled into the driveway, a radio announcer told the time: ten minutes after three.

I got out. The front door of the house was unlocked. Making sure I wasn't dripping slime, I went in.

The house was quiet and dark.

I heard a voice coming from the kitchen. Drago's. I entered the kitchen. He had his back turned and was talking on the cordless phone. I cleared my throat. He turned around, looked at me, and almost jumped out of his shoes.

Then said into the phone, "He just walked in . . . Yeah . . . No, I think he's okay. He just looks like he fell in a swamp and the swamp spat him back out. He smells even worse . . . Yeah . . . Well, I'll find out. I'll have him call you later."

Drago hung up. "That was your mother. We were starting to get worried about you. I can't wait to hear what the hell you've been into."

He didn't sound angry.

"Well, I—"

He shook his head and held up a hand. "No, I can't listen yet. You stink too much and you look cold. Go upstairs and take a hot shower. I'll make a fresh pot of coffee. Seahawks got their rear ends kicked today. You want a turkey sandwich?"

"I would love one."

"Shilo left me all these fresh turkey slices but I can't find the cranberry sauce. Where the heck does she keep the cranberry sauce? I've been looking for twenty minutes."

I pointed to a cupboard and headed upstairs to the shower.

It was one of the best turkey sandwiches I'd ever had. Oozing mayonnaise and cranberry sauce.

"If you can coach baseball half as good as you can make a sandwich . . ." I said, taking another bite and a swig of black coffee. I was wearing a pair of Jack's baggy sweats. Dick Drago was sipping a beer and chewing his sandwich. I told him what had happened, and he listened without saying anything.

"What did you do with the baseball?" he asked.

"It's in the front seat of my car. Want to see it?"

"Hell, no. Besides, I've got to be going. I have a long drive back to Shute, and I want to get over the pass before dark."

He stood up and went into the living room. I followed him. This was the most formal, unused room of the house. Drago had put his briefcase on the coffee table. With his thumbs he popped open the two brackets of the briefcase. Saying nothing, not looking at me, he reached in and pulled out a packet of papers. I was still standing at the steps that led down to the sunken living room, hesitant to enter the room, not so much because Drago was there but because Shilo always kept it off-limits. Drago put on a pair of Ben Franklin bifocals and flipped through the papers. I heard an airplane drone overhead. Then there was no sound.

Drago looked up from the packet, eyeing me through those bifocals. He seemed to relax a bit. He sighed, took a deep breath, held the letter of intent in one hand and a pen in the other, and said, "Decision time. What's it going to be, Mr. Duffy? Yes or no? What's it going to be?"